Crossing the Line

CROSSING THE LINE

Five connected theatrical monologues concerning child sexual abuse, trauma, and secondary victimisation. With explanatory notes.

Michael Sheath

Crossing the Line
Michael Sheath

Published by Aspect Design, 2022

Designed, printed and bound by Aspect Design
89 Newtown Road, Malvern, Worcs. WR14 1PD
United Kingdom
Tel: 01684 561567
E-mail: allan@aspect-design.net
Website: www.aspect-design.net

ISBN 978-1-912078-42-4

For Samuel Sheath (1921–2015)
and Beryl Sheath (1927–2010).
My mum and dad.

Contents

Foreword
Sarah Burrows, Director, Children Heard and Seen

Children Heard and Seen support children with a parent in prison in their own communities. The charity's specialised staff work with families to create a tailored wraparound package of support, offering one-to-one support with trained staff, volunteer mentoring, peer support groups for children, and more. Support is offered with a focus on raising aspirations, improving mental health outcomes, and breaking the cycle of intergenerational offending.

The monologues included in this book present a raw and thought-provoking exploration of themes of loneliness and isolation, as well as highlighting the rippling effects that crime and the legal system can have on the family members of those who commit offences.

The experience outlined in 'The Daughter' holds particular significance to us, as it is an experience shared by many of the families that we have supported. Although the father in the monologue did not ultimately receive a prison sentence, the trauma of arrest, police searches, public stigma, and separation are all felt by children of those convicted of sexual offences. The voices of children in these circumstances are so often invisible, and we are so pleased to see Michael shining a light on a child's perspective of loss as a result of parental offending.

We are so grateful to Michael for supporting our work and encouraging others to think about the experiences of children left behind.

Thank you.

Acknowledgements

Working for the Lucy Faithfull Foundation and Stop it Now! has been a privilege, and I would not have had that opportunity without Hilary Eldridge, the former director, taking a chance on me in 1997. Deborah Denis, the current director, has taken the organisation to a point most would never have thought possible in terms of the breadth and depth of its reach and influence. I thank both of them for having faith. Debbie Barlow has allocated work to me for twenty four of the twenty-five years of my tenure: the first year was chaos I'm sure. She often called me by her husband's name, and maybe we have spent as much time together. Thanks, chuck.

Debbie Jones of LFF won't thank me for thanking her because she is a model of modesty, moral probity and quiet competence, but she stepped in when I needed it. So did David Glasgow. Adrian Todd, formerly of West Mercia Police, and I experienced glamour and horror in equal quantities during our British Overseas Territory 'holidays', and I thank him for being there and suggesting I 'should have been a detective', which I found terribly flattering. I like to believe him.

Thanks to Jump Start, the Worcester arts project that provided the bump I needed, and to Joanna Lavelle, a great actress, whose enthusiasm for the original work and gentle demands for more of it meant the project finally took flight.

My wife, Janice, has been there for the entirety of my employment in roles that test the spirit. She has always loved, understood and supported me, even when I was on various edges, albeit metaphorical ones. I love her back. Morgana, our daughter, helped with suggestions and designs for the cover, and has taken far more notice of my doings than I suspected. It's always the quiet ones, I find.

Some hundreds of unnamed clients and police colleagues have inspired the work, I hope I have respected their stories and presented their experiences faithfully.

Note

What is this book?

It is a collection of five theatrical monologues, each of which can be read, or performed, as pieces of work in their own right. Most of the monologues have been performed or filmed already, and have engaged both lay and professional audiences. The pieces are meant to open the heart and also appeal to the intellect, and thereby facilitate an informed, honest and impassioned conversation about the themes they address. There is too much denial, ignorance and silence, still, about these matters.

It is also a collection of observations about sexual crime against children in the twenty-first century, and how the Internet and digital technologies have facilitated it.

It is also a reflection on trauma, and dealing with trauma, and survival, and redemption.

If you are not already familiar with any of this work, I would quietly suggest that you begin by reading 'The Wife' first, and then come back to the preface. I cannot think of a fancy term for 'plot spoilers', but skipping the preface at this point will allow you to miss them.

Preface

Crossing the Line is essentially about trauma, vicarious trauma, and collateral damage as they attach to child sexual abuse, be that in the online environment or otherwise. The work is based upon my observations of people and systems during ten years spent as a probation officer, from 1988, followed by twenty-five years working for a charity, the Lucy Faithfull Foundation. This UK based NGO describes itself as 'the only UK-wide child protection charity dedicated solely to preventing child sexual abuse.' The Foundation runs a helpline and website, 'Stop it Now!', which offers advice and counselling to individuals troubled by their own sexual thoughts and feelings about children, as well as individuals, usually partners or parents, concerned about the behaviour of others. My involvement has tended to have been after the event, when someone has been victimised, or when child sexual abuse material has been consumed. I have written hundreds of what are termed 'Expert Witness' reports to advise judges in the family courts; run groups for offenders and adult survivors; delivered training to police officers and social workers, and conducted enquiries into the safeguarding culture of whole communities in British Overseas Territories.

Thirty-five years is a long time. During that time I feel that I have been traumatised, vicariously traumatised, and collaterally damaged in my own right, although the writings here are a way of exploring the experiences fictional others undergo. My own experiences have been, I would say, trivial compared to the majority of the clients and communities I have worked with, but I hope they lend an authenticity to the expositions which follow. I have lost count, in truth, but I must have worked with, or had knowledge of, close on a thousand perpetrators of sexual abuse, probably five hundred women connected to those men, a few hundred police officers, and hundreds of children. Each has their own story, their own experience, and their own way of managing that. They have, I think, become embedded in my own memory. I have distilled all of their stories into five interconnected accounts, told from the first person, as monologues.

In December of 2015 I experienced public and professional shaming following the publishing of an enquiry into a project I had been involved in. I was explicitly and extensively criticised. I had lived with the knowledge that the day was coming for around nine months: an horrific and exhausting gestation characterised by a lack of sleep and an endless preoccupation with the inevitable outcome. The reality, if anything, was worse than I had anticipated. The nature of the project and the manner in which it ended do not matter here, but on one very dull and very miserable winter morning just prior to Christmas 2015 I stood on a railway platform in the north of England, and considered, momentarily, that these were the sort of circumstances in which someone might step off the platform onto the tracks at the moment when an express train was passing. I had no intention at all of doing so, the contemplation was academic, almost a detached exploration. The express passed, at speed, without incident. I sat on a cold bench and waited for my train.

Later, just days later I think, I saw an advertisement online that referred to an arts project called 'Jump Start.' This invited the submission of short dramatic works, of no more than twenty minutes duration, with the prospect of the work being performed in a small Worcester arts centre. I had not written any fiction since

I was at school, all of my writing since then had either been for academic purposes at university, or was prepared with a county court judge in mind. There could be few flourishes in that work, no imagination; everything had to be referenced and rooted and constrained by protocol. The idea of fiction, in that moment of my professional life, seemed liberating. The monologue, about a woman whose husband had been arrested for downloading child sexual abuse material was written in a matter of hours, with almost no edits, like automatic writing. I imagined a character, Geoff, the husband and downloader, who did not have allies or people whom he knew loved him, who had surrendered to shame, and who did not consider his self destruction in an academic way. I invested Diana, 'The Wife', with some of the puzzlement, anger, powerlessness and confusion I had experienced in my own life for some months. I sent it off with no expectations at all, for me the point was in the creation, the escape into imagination rather than the outcome. To my surprise, it was accepted for performance, and was performed in the spring of 2016. I deal with that process in a later chapter.

Two subsequent acts: 'The Mother', and 'The Detective' were written after a friend of my sister's, an actress, had performed 'The Wife' at an arts fringe festival and, a year later, asked for something that would make a performance of an hour. I had already started 'The Detective', and changed his gender so that a woman could perform it. Later, I changed it back, as I felt the interactions between the protagonists worked better with a male character in the role. During the first Covid lockdown of 2020 I wrote about Geoff, 'The Downloader' for that same actress. It was presented as his suicide note, read by Diana. I later changed it so that it could be acted directly, a monologue by Geoff. A year later I addressed the experience of Geoff and Diana's unnamed daughter, this following some interest from a charity, Children Heard and Seen, that works with the children of prisoners. Profits from this book, such as they may be, will go towards funding their vital work. If Geoff had lived, his daughter would have to bear the stigma of his imprisonment, as it was she had to manage something worse.

The parts are connected: Geoff, 'The Downloader', views child sexual abuse material; Diana, 'The Wife', has to bear the consequences of his arrest, and so does their child, 'The Daughter.' 'The Detective' arrests Geoff, and he has, previously, investigated a case of sexual abuse described by 'The Mother.' The implication is that Geoff has viewed images produced during the course of that abuse. My inspiration, I'm sure, was *Rashomon*, the 1950 Kurosowa film where four characters describe the same event from their own (and only) point of view.

It is difficult, in the abstract, to connect the behaviour of someone who has been prosecuted for being in possession of some ten thousand abusive images to a significant number of individual children, each of whom has a story of abuse to tell, if only they could tell it. Most of these children are never identified or helped; most of their abusers and the viewers of their abuse are never identified or punished. Child sexual abuse images are of real children, and their suffering needs bearing in mind during abstract discussions about 'viewing', 'downloading', and 'sharing.' By the same token it is difficult to imagine the impact of necessary police enquiries into abusive downloading upon the women and their children who are the secondary victims of it, or upon the detectives who have to investigate it.

I hope, through this work, to bring a louder voice to those who usually remain silent, or whisper.

The Wife

Diana is aged between thirty-five and forty-five. 'Respectably' dressed, maybe wearing a skirt and cardigan. She sits on a sofa, to one side, leaving a space for another person. There's a little table by the side of the sofa, with a glass of water on it. She addresses the audience as if she were talking to a friend or confidante.

It was about half past six in the morning. My brother works for them, you know, and he said they start a shift at six, so that would fit. I was asleep and there was this knocking on the door, not loud, but persistent: [*She knocks, in the air*] 'Tap tap tap tap tap. Tap tap tap tap tap.'

I thought it must be a mistake, no one calls at that time, my conscience was clear, as they say. I went downstairs, and I could see, through the frosted glass in the door, that there were three or four people there. It was too early for Mormons, or Jehovah's Witnesses, or anything else. They were all in suits. Somehow, I knew who they were. Before I could open the door I could hear Geoff, my, [*pause*] erm, husband, getting up. He was barging about his study, his office, upstairs. I remember thinking: 'What's he going in there for? At a time like this?'

I opened the door on them, [*Recalls*] four of them, a man and a woman, two other men behind, all with faces like they'd come to bring bad news. 'A deathogram', that's what my brother calls it, when he goes to someone's house, tells them their husband's dead in a car crash or something, but my husband was upstairs, banging about, so it couldn't be that. The children were in bed. The woman caught my eye as if she was about to say something, the man was looking at his shoes, the other two were stepping from one foot to the other, like they wanted to be somewhere else.

I was about to ask what it was they wanted when I saw they'd all started looking over my shoulder and Geoff was there, wearing this Simpsons dressing gown. Homer Simpson. Homer Simpson giving a big stupid thumbs up. The children bought it him for Christmas, or at least I gave them the money, and when they couldn't be bothered to go I picked it out, and I wrapped it, but they wrote on the label, after I'd nagged them. [*Smiles, shrugs.*] Anyway, Geoff was half way down the stairs, holding his lap top out in front of him, like he was offering it as a sacrifice, or surrendering it, with his stupid, stupid dressing gown on, the big stupid Homer Simpson thumbs up, the stupid Homer Simpson face, Geoff's stupid face now, like he had no idea what he was doing.

I was looking at him. God knows what my expression was. I had no idea what was going on, we might have stood there all morning as they didn't appear to want to say anything and I had no idea what it meant, this crowd of . . . police. Geoff broke the silence, and he called, past me, looking past me, to the police, in his best managing director voice: 'I think this is what you're looking for, Officers.' [*Impression of pompous business type, holds hands out in front of her*] Just like that, like he was doing them a favour, like he was handing over a lost puppy. Like he wanted to make it good.

Of the two in front, the man was obviously in charge, his face was blank, he stepped forward and took what Geoff was offering without a word, and he passed it back to one of the other men, who then backed out of the house. He started talking, the detective, but I can't remember the order of the words, there were a whole raft of things in there [*Makes quote marks*] 'indecent images', 'possession', 'children' 'you do not have to say anything.' It was like I could hear all these separate words, but I couldn't put them in a sentence, and I couldn't attach them, apply them, to my Geoff.

There was a lot of action after that. Geoff went to get some clothes on, one of the other men went with him, God knows what for, like he was going to throw himself out of the window or something. Ha! [*Pauses, sips water.*] And do you know what I did? At the same time as I was watching my whole, settled, untroubled life going down the toilet? I put the kettle on and I made them all a cup of tea.

Once they'd drunk it, Geoff left his to get cold, they were all in his office, putting all sorts of things he had in there in plastic bags, sealed them up, carried them out to the car, took him out to the car, put him in the back, away they went. One of the neighbours saw, but she was pretending she wasn't looking. We'd been round there at New Year, she was all 'Auld Lang Syne' then, not a bloody word since. I sat on the stairs with my head in my hands and my heart beating through my ribs. You know what they say about heartbreak? [*Appeals to front row*] I felt mine go, I really did. It's like an, ahmm, death, like a death, but you're still here aren't you?

The amazing thing was, looking back, our children didn't wake up. They got up for school, I took them as usual, waved them inside, and I went home and I cried and waited. I thought it was a mistake and that he'd be back, that they'd come to the wrong house. But he'd handed his computer over hadn't he? His face said there'd be something on it, in it, that he'd be ashamed of.

About two o'clock, two other people turned up, two women, from Children's Services they said. They 'strongly advised' me, those are the words, 'strongly advised' that Geoff should stay away, live away, until all this was sorted out and they could make sure the children were safe. I didn't do myself any favours. It was

nerves I guess, the shock. I laughed in their faces. 'Safe?' I said.
Well, I shouted, actually, 'Safe? My kids, well, his kids, our kids,
you're saying they're not safe with their own dad?' Well, one of
them wrote that down straight away, I could see she was pleased
with herself, pleased to have captured it, and she repeated it at a
meeting about a week later, like she'd got hold of the Holy Grail.
It indicated, she said, that I was 'not protective.' [*Mimes writing in
a notebook.*] 'We don't call it child pornography' they said, on the
visit, that first afternoon. 'We call it abusive imagery.' 'Have you
been on a course then?'[*Imperious*] I said, 'to learn that?' 'I know
what it is, you don't need to tell me.' They left soon after that, with
their notes, their contempt for me was written all over their faces. I
cried as soon as I shut the door on them, and I had twenty minutes
before I collected the children to get my face straight. [*Moves hand
across face, like a mime, produces a smile*]

Geoff didn't come back, anyway. He phoned me, said he couldn't
face me, and that he was staying with his sister until it was all
settled. 'Settled?' I said, 'What do you mean, what have you done?'
He couldn't answer, I could hear him crying, like a child, like a
forty five year old child.

He met me in the pub a few days later, after I'd had to persuade
him to see me. It was like a date, we joked about it before it happened,
we hadn't been out together, without the children, for about, what,
five years? I'd told the children that their dad was away, working,
somewhere. He'd been away before, quite a bit really, so they didn't
ask much, although they did ask why he hadn't said goodbye the
night before, and they did wonder why he didn't phone, like he
usually did. Of course, once we had 'Paedo!' spray painted on the
garage door I had to tell them. [*Pause*] But that came later.

He told me. He told me, he'd always been interested in
pornography. I'd always found it boring, or just stupid, or sexist

or whatever, so he'd kept it away from me. Early on, there'd been a couple of DVDs he brought home from somewhere, and he'd put them on the TV, and I'd said it wasn't for me, and that was that. Of course, [*pause, an aside, conspiratorial*] It's funny how I took on what he said isn't it? Of course, the Internet comes along, and it's all free, and he can watch what he wants in his office, one thing leads to another, he gets all these free offers, these links, these pop ups, and he's hooked. [*Shrugs*] Or so he says.

The two women from Children's Services asked me, like they were accusing me of being indifferent, or being complicit, if I'd noticed anything about him over the years he was doing it: he'd told the police, but he didn't tell me, even later, that he'd been breaking the law for five or six years before they arrested him. They told me that, like they knew him better than I did. Did I not know? Did I not notice? Didn't I see him looking at the children funny? Did he go off me? All that. I said I'd seen nothing, that he was the same, funny, loving man I'd married fifteen years ago, [*points finger at invisible social workers*] and that whatever filthy ideas they had in their minds about him, they were wrong.

[*Sighs, drinks water, pause*] Of course, it wasn't true. I mean, I wasn't going to give them any satisfaction. He had changed. I don't want to go into it, but he'd gone off me. I asked him, in the pub, on our date, whether he preferred porn to me, like it was another woman, a woman who was more available, more compliant, more . . . well, more sexy than me. It's hard, after having children, to keep the weight off, to be, you know, interested and interesting. He said that wasn't it, but he wouldn't say what it was. I sat there nursing my white wine, and he sat there nursing his beer, and we just . . . let it go. What I couldn't ask, and he wouldn't tell me, was about the children. The children in the films he'd seen. Were they like our children? Were they? Were they different? Foreign? Sexy? Can you have sexy children? [*Tone rises with each question*] I wanted to smash my glass in his face, but when I looked at how broken he was I just wanted to, to make it better, to agree he'd accidentally crossed a line. That was the phrase he used: 'Crossed a line.'

Between sips of my wine, £7 a glass it was, I was thinking: 'when we were, intimate, you know, were you thinking about me, or were you thinking about something else, someone else, about them?' I couldn't ask him, because I didn't want to know the answer, not that he'd have given one, he could hardly look at me as it was. He just said that he'd crossed a line, that phrase again, and that he shouldn't have, and that he knew that when they looked into his computer and his search history he'd be in a world of trouble, that no one he knew would want to speak to him again, including me, including the children. It was just a matter of time, six months, he reckoned, before he'd be back in to see them, and then he'd get charged. There was no way out.

I went home, after our 'date.' I was completely sober and none the wiser. Of course six months turned into nine, and he was charged. Possession, they called it, like it was drugs or something, and he said it was like that, like a drug that he couldn't stop taking at the same time as knowing it was destroying him, [*suddenly angry*]: It was always about him though, what he'd lost, how he felt, what was going to happen to him. I'd have to remind him, 'What about me? What about our children? What are we going to do?' I hadn't told anybody about it, as far as all our friends knew we were having some difficulties, he was at his sister's, that was that.

He'd visit the children, but I had to be there, and we'd sit in the one room, playing board games we hadn't played for years, and he'd catch my eye, like he wanted to say something, but I couldn't look at him. I just kept rolling the dice, moving the pieces, keeping up the chatter.

It was two days before he was due to be sentenced. He'd been in the paper. The garage door got sprayed with that word. [*Takes drink, takes a breath*]

It was in the evening, late on, too late for anyone to call round. The door knocked, that same knock as about a year before. I knew. I knew who it was going to be. It was the same detective, the same man, the same woman a pace behind him. They didn't need to speak. I knew the look, I'd said about it before, the 'deathogram.' He'd stepped in front of a train.

Once I'd finished screaming, and beating my hands on the chest of the detective, and cursing him for taking my husband from me . . . [*pause, recollects, shrugs*] he stood there like a statue. [*Baffled.*] I put the kettle on and made them a cup of tea.

Notes About 'The Wife'

'The wife' only acquired that title after I wrote 'The Detective.' The original piece was simply called *Crossing the Line*, and was just a single act, the dictates of the competition were for a single act play, of no more than twenty minutes duration, with minimal staging. I had no idea about play writing, direction, settings and what they call mise en scene in the film industry, so I imagined a single actor talking to the audience. In a way, I had been the audience for a single person, telling their story, for thirty-five years. A monologue was the answer.

I had been dealing with women in Diana's shoes for almost all of my career, women married to men who subsequently sexually offended, or who discovered their husband had a hidden conviction, or had allegations made against him. Since the turn of the century I had been dealing with women married to men who had been arrested for downloading child sexual exploitation material, CSEM in the professional parlance. We had determined, since the explosion of viewing, never to call it child pornography. That term was seen as minimising the content, suggesting consent on the child's part, titillation of sorts. Having seen a volume of it in my dealings with the police, I agreed: the men I dealt with were looking at terrorist content: the terrorising of children for adult entertainment.

In the UK, in 2022, around 850 men a month are arrested for possession of CSEM. If the police had more resources, they'd arrest more. The investigations are relatively straightforward, if only from a procedural point of view. Usually, intelligence is received that suggests a certain IP address has been identified as having been connected to a known site distributing CSEM, the IP address resolves to a physical address, the police visit, often early in the morning and perform what is increasingly termed 'the Knock.' Almost invariably, the man of the house admits responsibility. He is arrested. His 'devices': computer, phone, storage material and so on are seized. Sometimes, other family members have devices seized too, and his own and his family's universe implodes. Women describe the experience as traumatic, many experience the symptoms that characterise PTSD: nausea, nightmares, panic attacks, and physical manifestations, such as weight loss and heart palpitations. As Diana suggests, she 'felt her heart go.'

I gave Diana a name, not that she ever refers to herself by it, but I had in my mind a previously confident woman, bordering on privileged. She has led an untrammelled and largely untroubled life, she believes that only bad things happen to bad people; she is good, so she will be fine. I had known a few Dianas in my life, and a few Dianes, mostly from my childhood in the latter case, and it was always the Dianas who had the confidence and competence I wanted my character to have. My own folksie notion in respect to how a woman like Diana might manage an assault upon her assumptions about the world was later made legitimate by my reading about 'Shattered Assumptions Theory', which suggested the same thing: women who experience what Diana experiences are more savagely affected if their lives, to that point, have been trauma free. The belief that only bad things happen to bad people, and that a person who leads a good life will not be visited by terrible events is, of course, a comforting and false myth. Diana has to manage a tide of outrage and trauma that is not of her doing.

The first version of 'The Wife' had two detectives being

accompanied to the house by uniformed officers. Diana reports seeing 'two fluorescent jackets, badges, helmets' through the frosted glass of the front door. Feedback from police officers who saw a later filmed version of this act suggested this was inauthentic, that it was not standard procedure. Women like Diana I have spoken to suggested this was their experience, although latterly it seems to have become rare. The later version changed, if only to avoid a distraction, to have the police attending without uniforms and without liveried police vehicles. I am sure most people witnessing a cohort of men and women in suits attending a house at dawn can make a correct assumption as to what it means; there is no solution to that, it must be done.

The idea of Geoff's ridiculous and contextually jarring dressing gown came from my own life. I had a *Wallace and Grommit* dressing gown, and I imagined the incongruence of wearing it if anyone came to the door of my house in the early hours of the morning: the vulnerability of the situation amplified by the comedic nature of the clothing. Geoff's dressing gown, as with a number of elements of this first act, features in later acts, by way of different perspectives.

Diana's account, what she experiences, how she feels, and how she behaves, was based upon a distillation of some dozens of accounts of the same experience I had heard over two decades. There were certain commonalities: the sense of personal betrayal, the powerlessness, the stigma, the challenge to her own sexuality, or more accurately her attractiveness. Geoff betrays her by viewing indecent imagery and bringing her settled life to an end, he fails to offer any explanation as to his conduct, so leaving her mystified and powerless. Seemingly unsympathetic social workers challenge her understanding of her husband, and threaten her competence as a parent. The neighbours ignore her, someone spray paints her garage with what she calls 'that word.'

Despite all that, Diana attempts to bring normality, or as much normality as she can, to her children's lives. She attempts to maintain a relationship with Geoff, meets him for a drink to allow him an opportunity, an opportunity he fails to take, or simply cannot take, to explain his behaviour. She experiences the ambivalence that many of the women I have interviewed experience: she wants to make it better and she wants to punish him. She facilitates contact, obeying what she sees as the diktat of the Local Authority. She supervises, sits in, whilst the children play board games with their father. We learn from Geoff, later, his desperate attempts to communicate something to her. By that point she has decided to protect herself.

The time scale over which the first act takes place, just over a year, is not untypical: some police forces might take two or three years to progress a case from arrest to conviction, the technical side of the investigation takes time, the courts are overwhelmed with cases, even 'simple' possession cases with an early indication of a guilty plea become mired. In parallel to that process is the civil law: if a mother decides to end the marriage and resists the father's wish for contact with his children she may find herself contesting his application in a private law case; if she wishes to remain in the marriage and allow or wish for contact she may be seen as 'unprotective' or 'failing to protect.' If she denies the Local Authority's concerns she is seen as wilful, obstructive, uninformed; if she agrees with them but is disbelieved she may be regarded as engaging in 'disguised compliance.' If she is believed she is likely to be left with no support at all since she will be deemed as being 'a protective factor', this in the language of the standard formulations favoured by the bureaucracy. She may not, in all likelihood, be regarded as being a person in her own right.

In terms of local reaction, the neighbourhood's hostility, embarrassment or indifference, the newspaper reporting, the graffiti on the house were all based in reality. I dealt with a man once who was quietly confident he would not be 'outed' as he had moved house between his arrest and his sentencing, and he travelled a hundred miles or so to attend the Crown Court. On the way home from court his mobile phone began to light up with messages from his adult daughters. They had no knowledge of his arrest, but the fact of his sentence had been reported online, his unusual surname had been noted, and the facts were being broadcast on Facebook. They were aghast at his conduct and at his withholding the fact of it from them. By the time he returned home, to a leafy suburban road, the neighbours had printed out the online report, with a photograph, and nailed copies to every tree. Having slowed his car to a walking pace in order to read them he simply drove past his own home without stopping and returned to his parents. His wife joined him there, he had to explain himself to his daughters later.

I decided that Geoff should commit suicide early on in the writing process. The decision reflected some realities: between 3 per cent and 4 per cent of men on bail for possession of CSEM commit suicide, my organisation deals with that reality on a regular basis. A primary function of our Helpline has always been to provide an alternative: thoughts of suicide in the men who call are commonplace. In terms of the drama, I needed an ending, the original notion was of a single act, and I wanted a resolution. Of course, in real life, suicide is not a resolution, it is a commencement of sorts, albeit that the suicide himself is released from the consequences of his own choice: others pay the price. These issues were to be explored later.

It is no coincidence that Diana mentions death early on. Her reference to her situation being 'like death' mirrors Colin Murray Parkes' work on bereavement and a Barnardo's paper that compared the archetypal response to death to the response many women offer to discoveries of illegal and abusive downloading.

The revelation of Geoff's behaviour triggers her denial of his dangerousness, her anger at him and at the authorities, her sadness, her ambivalence, and the slow and tortuous nature of her eventual resignation. All those feelings mirror elements of loss before she has to deal with a real and shocking bereavement at the point of Geoff's violent suicide.

In terms of the play's first performance, I was entirely dependent upon others. One of the organisers of the Jump Start project offered to direct, he found an actor, and we had a read through in my house. I had little to offer, I knew how the words sounded in my mind, and anything approximating that would do.

The play was performed, with four others in the same competition, in the cellar of an arts building in Worcester. This was in the spring of 2016. The audience, possibly sixty in number, was primarily made up of the friends and relatives of the writers and performers. When my offering's turn came, I stood to one side, towards the back, and looked along the line of the audience. Diana offered her story to a silent and increasingly anxious audience: her experience was revealed, gradually and inexorably. I knew what was coming, but the final lines were, despite that, profoundly affecting. The performance was, I felt, both beautiful and terrifyingly real. I think I had decided to write another part before the play had ended.

A brief question and answer session at the end offered generic support and interest, and one very angry contribution, that I had failed to consider the children in the images, and that I had been too focused on, bordering on too sympathetic to, Geoff. I took the perspective to heart, and had in mind that my Detective (the idea of him as a character in his own right actually emerged during the performance) would offer a morally outraged counterpoint to Geoff's stubborn failure, at least in this first act, to appear penitent.

A final point. Many women in Diana's position do, in fact,

make tea for the police. Perhaps it is a form of denial, that this is a social call, perhaps it is an attempt to take control or take the initiative, to become a hostess. Scepticism about this detail is often offered by 'lay' audiences. Police officers nod or tap their colleague's shoulders in recognition.

The Detective

The Detective is a man in his late forties or early fifties. He's wearing trousers and a shirt, it looks a bit worn. He might be sitting next to a coffee table, there's a half empty bottle of vodka on the table, and a glass of vodka, quite full, that he sips from between some of the paragraphs. He doesn't tell us his name.

The Dirty Squad. That's what they used to call us. Stuck at the back of the station, overlooking the drains, overlooking the car park, overlooking the exercise yard. Some days, you'd have some nutter howling at the sky out there, it sort of added to the ambience. Other days, we'd watch the chief's secretary park her car, for light relief. She was terrible at it, [*shakes head in recollection, laughs*] she used to take the door mirrors off half the patrol cars. The Dirty Squad, because we dealt with sex cases. I did it for five years before the noughties, thought it would be a good way to get some detective time under my belt, get out of uniform, get off nights, spend some time at home with my wife at the weekends.

They were simple times, kind of. You'd get a complaint, what they called a 'disclosure', from some kid, or from some woman. The adult rape calls would always come in on Monday. My sergeant used to put the phone down, once he'd taken the details and he'd go 'Ah, another weekend of regretted sex', and he'd allocate it to one of us, me or one of the women. It was seen as a woman's job, and it usually went nowhere. 'He says, she says', we used to call them.

Nine out of ten times you'd get the bloke in and he'd say she said yes, she'd say she said no, or said nothing 'cos she was too scared to speak, and that'd be it. Most times there's no marks of violence, no weapon. Just what he said. And what she said. And me, in the middle. And somebody's lied.

It's funny isn't it? Well, not funny, odd, that you can get life for it, a life sentence, for rape, if you're convicted, and the only difference is consent. It's a big difference, I know, but what other crime hangs on a word or two? I mean, if you burgle a house you can't possibly think the people that live there don't mind. Punch someone in the face, same thing. Sex becomes rape if the person on the receiving end, the woman in most cases, says that's what it is, or experiences it as that. Don't get me wrong, I investigated dozens of them, I can think of one or two where it didn't add up. In most of them it did and the man would walk away from it, the rapist I mean, and that'd be that.

The cases with kids were easier, and more difficult. I mean, they can't consent can they? That's what the law says, under sixteen, you can't consent, even if you sign an affidavit to say you were gagging for it, not that anyone ever did. So usually, no witnesses, no forensics, it was all on what you could get him to admit. Some blokes, they'd deny everything and keep their face straight, some men would say they'd been led on, and once they said that, that was it, guilty. If they didn't have a lawyer I might sort of lead them that way, say I understood how kids these days knew all about sex, might not say no. I'd try to catch their eye, get them on side, suggest I understood, with a raised eyebrow, get them to agree. I never knew whether the ones who admitted really believed they'd been led on, or whether it was an excuse. At the time, I didn't really care. A cough was a cough.

I'd have to do the interviews with the kids, they usually got me in to do the ones with the younger kids, they said I had a kind face, they reckoned the kids might talk to me. You'd have to make sure they understood the difference between truth and lies, build rapport, get a 'free narrative account' [*makes quote marks*]. Build rapport, that was a laugh, build rapport in a room with two cameras and a load of microphones, with a couple or three people watching on a remote TV. Once or twice, they'd be telling me what had happened and I could hear their mum, through the wall, wailing. People don't know this, don't want to know this, but 'Stranger Danger' is mostly bollocks. The kids I saw had all been abused by someone they knew, someone they liked, someone their mum liked. It's a trust thing, isn't it?

Anyway, five years of that and I'd had enough, so I went into CID, 'proper crime', Ordinary Decent Criminals we called them, as opposed to the Nonces, as in nonsense cases. I did all sorts, got a commendation or two. Did the drugs squad, the uniforms would put a few doors in with the magic key, this great metal battering ram, we'd all pile in, shouting. After a bit I realised I was doing the same doors, they'd only just put the hinges back on, fixed the frame, before we put it in again. You'd wonder, in the end, if there was any point, after a few years half the people I'd arrested were dead anyway. It's like they were playing Russian roulette but they'd put five rounds in the chamber instead of one. I felt bad for their kids.

In 2011 they started this new team, On Line Sex Crime Investigation, OLSCI for short, and I was straight in there, they made me the sergeant of it. It was all the online stuff, sex stuff, the groomers, the downloaders, the sextortionists, the exhibitionists, the paedophiles, all the weirdness you could find, there was no end to it. When I was in The Dirty Squad there was hardly anyone on the Internet, couple of geeks I knew, sharing software tips or photos of steam trains, you know? By the time I came back to it the net was awash with the porn and the child porn, with kids being raped in the live streams, with blokes creeping about looking for kids on Snapchat, Instagram, WhatsApp, Twitter, Movie Star Planet [*smiles, raises eyes to the ceiling*], whatever, making comments, making connections, asking for selfies, and getting them. Every now and again the chief would say we had to do something, so we'd go online, pretending to be kids, and you'd have to beat them off with a virtual stick. As soon as you'd pop up on some places, with a profile photo of one of the team in a swimming costume when she was twelve, you'd get this stream of comments: 'Are you horny? 'Sexy photo?' 'Want to see what I've got?' It was like fish in a barrel. I felt we were doing some good, making the Internet a safer place, taking out the bad guys. By that time I was divorced, had kids I only ever saw at the weekend, and I took it personally.

Operation Umbrella. Operation Umbrella was what finished me. Twenty-seven thousand names on a list, twenty-seven thousand IP addresses accessing a site in Romania, twenty-seven thousand men, as it turned out, and we had to Hoover them up one at a time. My team had a list of three hundred odd. Where to start? With the teachers, of course, plenty of teachers, and the football coaches, plenty of them too, and the dads, blokes with kids of their own, can you imagine? Blokes bringing up kids one minute, and looking at pictures of kids being raped the next: not their own kids, someone else's kids, like it makes a difference. Anyway, once we'd risk assessed them we did them in alphabetical order, it just seemed to make sense. If your name began with A you were going to get a visit straight off, if you were Mr Zebra or something it would have to wait.

Geoff Adamson was one of the first. It was pretty straightforward, we knocked his door at zero dark hundred, having squeezed passed the two Audis on the drive. I remember the look on his wife's face, she opened the door, stood there with her mouth wide open, he was coming down the stairs in a cartoon dressing gown with his lap top. He looked ridiculous. He knew who we were and why we were there, they usually do, and he handed his computer over like he thought it would make us go away, satisfied. His wife sort of melted inside, I'd seen it so many times, but she remained upright, made us tea, I'd seen that before too. Once he'd put his clothes on he just sat on the sofa with his eyes bulging with unspent tears whilst my lot searched his office.

Once we got him in an interview room, and I managed to persuade him to stop crying, the tissues piling up on the table, he offered the usual tale of the slippery slope, told us how guilty he felt, how much he wanted help, how he was glad we'd arrested him, how he was a porn addict who'd crossed a line. We sent his computer off to the geeks for analysis, same with his phone, and they were both riddled with it, child porn, abusive images, I mean.

Part of the job, [*looks uncomfortable, pauses*] part of the job was to look at what he'd looked at, to grade it, we called it, write descriptions of what was in the image, in the picture, in the film, so that when it came to court the judge could get an idea. It was to help sentencing: the worse it was, the longer he'd get. I'd put headphones on so my team couldn't hear the kids crying, but I [*emphasis*] had to keep my eyes open and my ears open, and at the end of the shift I'd be sitting there with nothing on the screen and nothing in my ears . . . and I could still see it, and I could still hear it. That was how it worked, three hundred names on a list, hundreds of thousands of images, a year looking into this pit, this pit of filth and horror and dealing with these men, most of them crying in the interview room, and me wanting to smash their faces in because the kids in the pictures looked like my kids and they looked like their kids and they looked like the kids I'd spent hours with in that bloody interview room almost twenty years before: they all began to blur.

The thing with Geoff Adamson was, well, his wife's brother worked in traffic, and I knew him, we'd been on the drug squad together, he was a good bloke, a good copper, and he told me Adamson was a good bloke too, a good husband, a good dad, and that he wasn't your typical sex case. We shouldn't have had that conversation, but Adamson was stone cold guilty, he'd put his hands up on day one, the file was with the CPS and off my desk, so I let it go. There were dozens of cases the same though, ordinary men, ordinary men doing terrible things online, and their hands were dirty. I'd tell them that in the interview: 'You can't say you're only looking, that it's only pictures, you've got dirty hands, you're complicit.' Some of them understood, most of them just looked broken, or they'd stare back at me like I was speaking a language they couldn't understand.

The more men I met, the more men I arrested, the more they seemed like men I knew, and I began to feel sorry for them, but the more images I had to grade, the more I hated them, and the more I had in my head that I couldn't shift. The day Adamson was in court for plea, there was a bloke from the paper there, and before he'd even left the court it was online, in the online paper, and then it was on Facebook, and someone spray painted his house with the word 'Paedo.'

I had to go round there, reassure his wife, although I couldn't really offer her anything: I knew he'd get jail in the end, and so did she. I knew his kids would get stick at school, and I looked at their photos on the piano, in their expensive frames, and I thought 'your lives are messed up, and I knocked the door, I sort of put your door in, and nothing's going to put it back on its hinges. Nothing's going to fix the frame.' It was just like the drug squad, I was wondering what the point was.

My last day at work. [*Pause, pours vodka, drinks*] Cheers. I was in the office, they'd put my shiny new team in the old Dirty Squad office, I was looking out of the window, at the car park, judging the reversing, listening to the prisoner bellowing 'Who let the dogs out?' The phone rang, some uniform guy, he'd been called out to the train station, they'd scraped this man off the tracks, horrible mess, he had my card in his pocket, one of my sex cases. Geoff Adamson. I said I'd deal with it, deal with the visit, so I went up there, though I didn't want to, after I'd seen him in the morgue, to deliver what must never be referred to as 'the deathogram.'

It was late on, and as soon as she opened the door I knew that she knew, and that didn't make it any easier because I felt it was my fault, that if we'd started at *Z* and worked our way backwards instead of *A* and gone forwards there was a chance he might have stopped, or at least deleted everything, somehow, by the time we got round to him, and I wouldn't have had to wreck his life and his kids' lives and his wife's life. And once I'd told her what she already knew, that he was dead, she flew at me, and she was actually beating on my chest, screaming and cursing me, and saying I'd killed her husband, and I deserved it, because it was sort of true.

Once she'd stopped screaming she actually made us a cup of tea, and I went home. I sat there in the dark. I could still see all these kids that were abused for Adamson's entertainment, I could see his smashed body on the mortuary slab, I could see all these broken men who were just like men I knew, and I could hear Adamson's wife screaming, and the kids in the films screaming, and the faces of his kids in the expensive frames on the piano, and I downed a bottle of vodka, near enough, like I'd been doing every other day of the week, and I put my Warrant Card in the bin, and I never went back.

Notes on 'The Detective'

I wanted the Detective to illustrate the tensions that exist in relation to investigations into the possession of CSEM. I also wanted him to exemplify, to illustrate, the impact of dealing with the horrors he has to deal with on a daily basis. Sexual abuse, trauma, vicarious trauma, and burnout are essentially the themes of the five monologues, and the Detective is another vessel through which they are explored. There was no need to give the Detective a name, so he simply exists. Like Inspector Goole, who is named, albeit falsely, in *An Inspector Calls* he offers a correct and moral analysis of what he experiences; he and 'The Mother' are connected in that role. I imagined, in my own mind, that it was this detective who dealt with her daughter Leanne's experience of grooming so compassionately. It is the mother he refers to, without knowing, as someone he could hear crying through the wall of the ABE suite when he is interviewing her child. She speaks of him being a nice man with a kind voice. We are later reminded, by her, of his professionalism and humanity.

Police officers tread a difficult path between investigating crime, safeguarding children, and causing families to implode. Of course, some men who view and collect CSEM are unambiguously dangerous to children. Other men viewing the same material are breaking the same laws and have 'dirty hands' as the Detective puts it, but their direct risk to their own children, at that point, remains unknown. At the point of 'The Knock', when police officers make an arrest, they typically have no idea who they are dealing with:

at the end of some investigations those mysteries remain. Mao, I think, spoke of guerrillas living like fish in the sea of the people. Child molesters swim in the same sea as the CSAM viewer, the groomer, the nihilistic pornography viewer and the desperate and undifferentiated consumer of brutal content.

There is, of course, unambiguous suffering involved in the production of Child Sexual Exploitation Material: an early and still useful Interpol definition I adopted for use in training events suggests that it 'depicts and promotes' child sexual abuse. 'Depicts', because it shows children being sexually abused, and requires them to be, 'promotes' because there's an ideological underpinning to it, propaganda in a way, a Siren call to the viewer to view more, engage more, enjoy more.

When the first viewers of CSEM on the Internet were identified in the mid 1990s they were often 'old school' paedophiles, collaborating in the dissemination of what they called 'kiddy porn' that was produced in the 1970s. The 2022 reader may be astonished to learn that this material was legally produced and sold, in magazine form, at that time. The tone was more 'Health and Efficiency', nudism, and quasi romantic notions of 'man boy love' than the unambiguously abusive, sadistic and exploitative material that came in the digital age, but the ideological underpinnings were the same: children were erotic and sexual objects, adults were entitled to sexual engagement with them or to find distraction and fulfilment in their nakedness, vulnerability, or abusive experience.

The Detective talks about the pre-Internet era of child exploitation I was familiar with: my career began in the pre-Internet era, in the late 1980s. It continued into the Internet era: I observed at close hand how rare the possession of CSEM was amongst the sexual offenders I worked with as an ingenue probation officer, and how ubiquitous it became later. In 1990 or so I dealt with one man who was found to have been abusing boys he taught; he had spent what, at that time, was a relative fortune on a VHS cassette with 'vintage' CSEM on it. Ten years later he could have found the same material in an online forum or a Peer to Peer network for free, and it would have been regarded in those quarters as comical and nostalgic.

Once the Internet became awash with pornography, and in truth it seems that the pornography industry rejoiced in, invested in and colonised the Internet, then the opportunities to find and view CSEM also became manifold. Digital cameras were used in domestic settings. The absence of scrutiny reduced shame, the absence of shame removed the inhibitions the curious and the ambivalent may have had about seeking out CSEM, the slippery slope and the blurred lines between 'teen' and 'child' fell away, for some, altogether.

I had been involved with police officers through my work in the Probation Service since 1983. When I worked in a Probation hostel they saved me from a beating on a few occasions. Once I qualified as a Probation Officer in 1988 I delivered some training in what is grandiosely termed 'offender profiling' and what one Australian detective of my acquaintance later termed 'how paedos think', which was technically inaccurate and off message, but I got his point. By the same token, the phrase 'dirty squad' came from a real world conversation I had with an acquaintance who investigated sexual crime in the 1980s. The language the police use can jar in polite company, but they can be forgiven for it in many cases. If you're dealing with what they deal with, and with the frustrations that come with that, then you deserve a bit of leeway as to how things get described: dark humour is a trait of those who work with dark forces.

Child molestation evokes strong and violent feelings in the bystander, and offensive and stigmatising language is used throughout the system as a means by which individuals deal with those horrors. I worked in a prison in the mid-1990s for two years, attached to the 'Rule 43' wing, which was inhabited by the sexual offenders and those being bullied who could not manage what was termed 'normal location.' My walk to the wing took me past those locations. Prisoners there knew where I was going, so I tended to be greeted with cat calls and abuse from the windows: 'Nonce!' or 'Beast!' were typical, although those who recognised my role, the suit and the keys on a chain were a clue, might shout 'Nonce Master!', which was what some of the prison officers called me. 'The Nonce Master's here' would herald my arrival on the wing. I tended to laugh, I had to fit in, at the same time as feeling compromised by doing so.

The Detective's account of his rape investigations, and his sergeant's description of 'regretted sex', again, come from real life. So does the phrase 'he says, she says', which is, in most cases, all a jury has to go on. Research on juries suggests they are likely to adhere to rape myths in any event: women who are not physically injured during the course of the alleged rape are regarded with suspicion. I wanted my detective to offer that depressing reality as his reality, but for him also to suggest that his view was that the majority of men he investigated were responsible for what had been alleged; that frustration would lie at the heart of his disenchantment. Complaints of adult rape are rare compared to the amount of experienced rape. Prosecution rates following complaints of rape in the UK have been in low single figures for some years now, and conviction rates following prosecution are just as low. The same applies to the experience of, reporting of, and conviction of instances of child sexual abuse.

Possession of CSEM is, by contrast, relatively easy to prove: the computer reliably and blindly records what it has seen. Denial of possession is usually futile and forensically disproved. Online

solicitation is, again, a relatively straightforward crime to prove.
Men engage children on social media sites, on gaming sites and via
popular Applications with a view to persuading them to provide
sexual images, or to meet 'in real life' or 'IRL'. The undercover
detective I met at his work station in The Met told me he only
'allowed' himself to be engaged by men he believed lived in London;
there were so many of them he did not need to cast himself further
afield. He wore a hat when he wanted to remember he was meant
to be acting as a child, and took it off to speak to me.

The Detective is changed by what he sees and experiences. It is
simply true that, prior to the emergence of the Internet, the only
people who saw children being sexually abused were those involved
in abusing them. After the Internet, literally millions of individuals
have seen those experiences, either deliberately and for pleasure or
distraction, or as, in the Detective's case, because it is part of his
duties. I do not think we have considered the cultural impact of
this phenomena enough. I knew a detective working in the field of
victim identification who wore headphones so that his colleagues
would not have to hear what he heard, he did not explain how he
managed the impact on himself. Victim identification officers analyse
seized images for clues as to the identity of the child, they become
experts in carrier bag logos, crisp packets, blurred baggage ticket
stubs, school uniforms, vehicle types, plug sockets and even tree
species, emerging from hours of scrutiny of three or four images
with the suggestion that the child may be in Romania, Laos, or a
certain state in the United States. In terms of sexual content they
see things, it is their duty to see things, that most people would
seek to avoid, save for men like Geoff.

The Detective is not involved in victim identification, so he
does not experience the occasional triumph and true sense that he
is responsible for a child being rescued and a perpetrator brought

to account. Instead, he 'grades' images, a task that is increasingly being automated so as to spare the viewer from the contaminating effects of exposure to hundreds of rape scenes. His seeing what the men he arrests have seen leads him, quite legitimately, to hate them for it, he wants to do them harm, if only in his imagination. When he arrests them his observation of their weaknesses, their lack of awareness, their lack of empathy and their inarticulacy on interview leads him to feel both puzzlement and pity.

Inevitably, over nearly three decades of work, I had been aware of police officers 'going under.' Sometimes it was just that 'DC this' or 'Sergeant that' wasn't in the role he or she had occupied any more. Nothing was explicitly stated. Sometimes they were men or women I had worked alongside, or trained with, and I knew they had left the service or had been reassigned because they could not continue to do what they had been doing, and cited the toxic nature of the material as being at the heart of that. Compulsory counselling had been forced upon them, but the workplace culture was that this interfered with 'doing the job', and that police officers needed to be tough enough to endure whatever came to them without complaint. Others have described counselling as 'parking an ambulance at the bottom of the cliff', since it identifies psychic damage after it has already been done.

I had heard a number of police officers draw the same comparisons to drug users as my detective offers. Initially, at the turn of the millennium, police seemed confident that they were invariably arresting men who posed a direct risk to children, the viewing of CSEM was diagnostic of paedophilia, paedophilia was diagnostic of child molestation. Over two decades those orthodoxies have been challenged, police officers found themselves dealing with men like themselves, 'good blokes, good husbands, good dads' to all observation, whose offending seemed, dare they say it, out of character.

Suicide rates amongst men arrested for possession of CSEM have been such that a report was commissioned as to how they might be reduced, this in 2017. It discovered a rate of just under 4 per cent in one significant operation, one suicide for every twenty five arrests. Whilst I have seen, on social media, whoops of delight when men under investigation kill themselves, I have yet to hear them from police officers: it is they, of course who have to deal with the consequences. Almost all the police officers I speak to on training events have three or four anecdotes to offer, all refer to the impact of suicide on the children, the wives, and their own morale.

Alcohol seems to be the drug of choice of the police: its communal consumption cements the sense of identity and camaraderie, the feeling that only police officers can know what it is to be a police officer. The Detective drinks alone, eventually, because he cannot share what he feels or what he has seen with others. There are hundreds of individuals in the same position: police, technical staff, and digital forensic investigators, all managing what they see and hear in their own ways, typically un-thanked, invariably under paid.

The Detective draws our attention to his uncertainty as to the point of his work, is 'the war on drugs' comparable? How many doors need be knocked? How many more doors will be knocked? In week one of my rather shaky social work education we were told the tale of a man picnicking by the river whose day is interrupted by his having to wade into the current to rescue drowning children. After a while, his curiosity finally aroused, he walks upstream to find that someone is throwing the children into the torrent. The lecturer paused to ensure we got the point: we might spend our career rescuing neglected or abused children rather than addressing the systemic causes of their condition.

The question I wanted to offer was not: 'Is it worth investigating CSEM offences?' I am firmly of the view that it is, that men who view images of child rape have to be held to account, and they have to desist. Any ambivalence I have relates to the collateral damage, the iatrogenic harms caused, or at least not minimised by the system itself.

The Detective has already begun to question his role before the act ends, he girds himself to visit Diana for a final time to tell her that her husband is dead, he accepts her curses and her assault upon him because, in part, he feels he deserves them. He resolves his own ambivalence as to the purpose of his role by resigning, his symbolic binning of his Warrant Card, the symbol of his authority whilst inebriated and (inappropriately) wracked by guilt.

The Downloader

Geoff: mid to late forties, wearing a suit without a tie. He's sitting at a table, there's a pen and some paper and envelopes in front of him. Mostly composed, occasionally resentful and exasperated, he is resigned to what the audience knows is coming.

I knew they'd come for me in the end. Even when I was at my most confident, most in control, there was always a feeling I was running out of road, and that sooner or later there'd be this... fall from grace.

When it came I wasn't ready. I was asleep and dreaming, next to my wife, ah, Diana. My wife was in the dream, and the kids, we were in a rowing boat, on a lake somewhere. It was one of those childhood memories I had of being with my parents, my father was rowing, my mum giving instructions, laughing. The oars were bumping against the... rowlocks? Is that what you call them? He wasn't very good at it, never improved. Anyway. In my dream I'd taken the place of my father, and I was rowing, and I was looking at the wife and the kids, and the oars were bumping against the... things, and then I was waking up and the bumping noise had turned into a knocking noise. The motion of the boat was shifting somehow into the bed lurching and I realised Diana was getting up, but it was dark, and there was someone at the door. And I knew.

She was downstairs before I could get there, and I could hear the voices in the hall, confident sounding on the doorstep, my wife's voice an octave higher, quizzical, panicked, but nothing compared to the state I was in. I thought my guts were going to heave out of me, somehow.

Like I said, I knew they'd come, and I knew what they'd want, so I grabbed my laptop from my study and carried it downstairs, out in front of me, like a shield it occurred to me later, or a sacrifice. Because my wife was at the bottom of the stairs I had to pass it over her head, and as I did so I looked at her mystified face, completely mystified, she was the only person there that didn't know what this was about.

It was all very polite. I remember thinking that maybe my giving them my computer, a Toshiba it was, nothing special, it would take the stain away, remove the crime and it would be okay. Maybe they'd be satisfied.

That's not what happened. It was more like the lurch in my guts was the same as you get when the roller coaster gets to the top of the track, and there's that moment of silence, of inertia, and then you're over the hump and gravity takes over. And there's no stopping it.

Once they'd focused on me, they gave me the caution. It was just like a TV programme except that I was in it. They went up into my study and were poking about in all the drawers. I kept saying that everything I had was on the computer, but they'd heard that one before, and they collected up all these old DVDs, memory sticks, those little video tapes of my children when they were babies, all that, and they put them in plastic bags, sealed them at the top, and carried them out to their cars. My wife made them all a cup of tea, she sort of went into hostess mode, I loved her for it at the time. Looking back, I wish we'd been less cooperative, fought back somehow. The process was so restrained, so, erm, English, repressed. They were killing me, and drinking my tea.

The detective was alright. The others obviously thought I was a pervert, a paedo, I could see it in their eyes, hear it in the hard

tone of their voices as they put me in the back of the car: 'In you
go, sir, don't bang your head.' The car was a Vauxhall I think, plain
colour to blend in I suppose, but the situation stood out a bit in the
cul de sac. Jean, over the road, popped her head out, sort of waved,
and then realised there was something off about it. Me, two men
in suits, a load of evidence bags, and her face froze in amazement.
'Tell your Bridge Club about it' I thought, nearly shouted it in fact.
She probably did. I felt naked, uncovered. Exposed.

I told the detective, in the privacy of the interview room, that
I'd been doing it for years. This was between bouts of crying, I
couldn't help myself. I said it was a relief to get caught, and it was,
at the same time as it wasn't. If I had a choice, and I had no choice,
I would have liked to have stopped doing it without getting caught.
But the time for that choice had gone. He told me he'd heard it
all before, wasn't judgemental at all, but he had the confidence of
someone who knew he'd got me cold anyway.

I could tell that in some ways he was acting, like play acting
the part of a detective, doing what you see them do on all those
shows. Except his heart wasn't in it, there was this resignation to
him, like he'd seen too much and I was just something else that
was adding to the horror of it. That made it easier to tell him the
worst of it, the tape was running, the counter rolling on, I was in
there for about two hours, he hardly said a word, just raised an
eyebrow every now and again to keep me going, passed over a tissue
so I could wipe my eyes, blow my nose, the tissues piling up on the
desk, damp, vile things.

By the time we'd finished I felt like I'd been in confession, I'd
confessed to pretty much everything I'd done; he said they'd look
on my computer, see what was on there, and then he let me go. I
thought, for a minute, that I'd be going home, but he'd already
told Social Services and said there was no way they'd allow it, and

anyway, he would only give me bail if I went somewhere there were no children. It was the only time I got angry, 'You think I'd do that to my kids?' I said. 'I'd rather chew my own arm off.' He was calm, implacable. I had to call my sister, explain what I'd done, and she took me in.

Telling my wife was harder. Well, I didn't really tell her anything, she knew as much as I could bear her to know, she'd been there when I'd been arrested of course, and later some social workers had told her I was a threat to the children, and why. We met for a drink a few days after I was arrested. Some kind of date, my wife said, which was bizarre, but there was this void between us. She said everything she thought about me was suddenly false. I was a puzzle to her. We sat there, in a pub we'd never been to before, and I kind of stared at my pint, looking for inspiration in the dark amber gloom of it. She sat there looking at this glass of wine she'd bought, the condensation on it slowly trickling down, the glass clearing, she hardly touched it. Some kind of date.

What was I supposed to tell her? Men like porn don't they? You see, when you're on there, on the net, how much of it there is. There has to be a demand, supply and demand, you don't need twenty years in accountancy to tell you that. Before the net I'd have the odd magazine, the odd DVD, but I was embarrassed to buy them, wouldn't go in a shop, a sex shop, to buy them. They used to call them 'dirty book shops', 'dirty films', it was pretty obvious, for dirty men. With the net there was anonymity, no shame, it felt like Christmas Day, every day, no waiting for next year for another present. Something popped up every day I was on there, and in the end I was on there every day.

You know what? Some of the legal stuff was pretty brutal: 'pounding this', 'destroying that', 'wrecking her', this was always on the menu. I know they have some sort of algorithm, once you get into that stuff they send you more of it, highlight it, suggest something similar but a bit harder.

The first time I saw something, erm, involving children, I swear to God, was an accident. I'd been on a teen thing, but it was fake, women dressing young, but there was this link on it and I clicked it, and I was looking at kids, some of them not much older than my daughter, *ppphhhhhwwww*. I shut it down straight away, actually slammed the lap top shut, but five minutes later, once my heart had stopped pounding, I opened it again and went back there. It was like [*long pause, genuinely struggling to find the word*] . . . a magnet. It's hard to remember now, but that balance between being appalled at what I saw, and being amazed at what I could see began to shift, and after a few weeks, months maybe, I was deliberately looking for it, and what I couldn't imagine looking at a few weeks before soon became something I was bored with.

I knew. I knew that if I told my wife everything that would be it. She wasn't a prude, but kids? Christ. I did enjoy some of it, or the ape in me did, call it what you like, but I swear to God it wasn't going anywhere. I had these two worlds going on, like on the net there were no rules and no decency and no compassion, but outside of that I was just a man, a dad, a husband. A bad one I know, but it was like my arrest kicked down the barriers between the two worlds. The police might just have well as kicked my door in instead of knock on it, like I was a gangster instead of . . . instead of whatever it is I am.

My wife said to me on our weird date, I could hardly say anything, my shame closed down on me like a narcotic, I sort of shrank into myself. Anyway, she was pretty composed, or numb. She said to me that what I'd done to her and the children was a crime, and she said what I'd done to the kids in the films and the pictures, even at one remove, by watching them, meant I was implicated in their abuse, and I was as guilty as the men that did it. There was nothing I could say, so I said nothing, just felt the pressure of tears behind my eyes, saw the confusion and the sadness and something like rage in hers. I knew she was right at one level, and I was ashamed, of what I'd done and of what I'd thought. And I knew, once the police got into my computer, into the belly of the beast, that the filthy and appalling totality of what I'd done would be there to see.

I saw the children a few times, at the house, but Diana had to be there in case I sexually abused them. Can you imagine the sort of bureaucratic mind that imagines these things? The children didn't know why I wasn't living at home, they just waited at the window until I drove up, and waved at the window as I drove away. I had these stickers on the back window of my car. Little stick people, one for me, one for the wife, two children, all in a row. Every time I looked in the mirror they were there, waving, mocking. I thought about scraping the damn stickers off, but then I thought: 'What if I just scraped myself off?', my thoughts began to drift, slowly, unstoppable, towards doing just that.

In the ninety minutes between my arriving and leaving we'd play bloody Uno, or Junior Cluedo, or Buckaroo, the one with the donkey that kicks all the stuff off his back. It was mine as a child, I'd looked after it, and it used to make my father laugh like a child when we played it, but I dreaded the thing going off as my children would laugh and cheer, which grated on my nerves, as I knew there was nothing to cheer about. I'd be staring into the side of my wife's face, trying to communicate my desperation to her. But she wouldn't look over, fifteen years of marriage, one mistake, and she cut off from me. It was like a door had closed and she was on the other side of it.

When I finally got to court, this was months later, they adjourned for reports, and by some process, I swear there was no reporter in there, it was in the paper, and then it was on Facebook, and someone spray painted the garage with 'Paedo', even managed to spell it right, so they must have been local. That pretty much decided it for me.

I'm calm about it now, the dread has faded a bit because I know this is going to get finished on my terms. I'm supposed to get sentenced on Friday. Previously I was in a dead panic about how it would turn out: divorce would follow my sacking would follow my public humiliation would follow my jailing. They say that once you make the decision your mind clears and you don't worry any more. There's lots of savings, the house is paid off. Diana will be better off without me. I think she's switched off from me, and this, now. I need to put a full stop on it. The kids. I love my children, but I'm no father to them now, not like I was. And I'm pretty sure they won't let me be one again. Let them remember me as I was; I've got nothing to offer.

I won't do it at my local station, I know too many people there, the regulars. I can just get off a stop later and do it there. I heard they give the driver a week off to deal with the trauma. I'll leave him a note too.

Notes on 'The Downloader'

Although I must have met or dealt with cases involving two or three hundred men who have been convicted for downloading, I found Geoff's part the most difficult to construct. It might be a matter of empathy, or a wish to avoid spending too much mental effort attempting to put myself in the shoes of a man who might do what he did. I suggest, in training events, that police officers and social workers have to get 'behind the eyes' of downloaders, to inhabit their world for a moment, to understand what drives them. I found myself taking longer to write from Geoff's point of view because I could not find where to pitch him. Was he actually abusing his children? Was he a fully fledged paedophile? Was he, as he told Diana, someone who had simply crossed a line?

There was, of course, no shortage of men upon whom I could model him. Very early on, between, say, 1990 and 2000, I met no end of men who would, unbidden, characterise themselves as paedophiles, it was not an insult to them, it was simply an identity, an accepted sexuality. They adopted an ideological stance that suggested they were victimised by society rather than that they were victimising others. They wrote disparagingly, and some online groups still do, about 'normies': people who do not share their world view. Normies are repressed, illiberal, conservative, moralistic, engaged in a fruitless war to prevent children from expressing their sexuality how they wish. Of course, the self confessed paedophile tended to fantasise that children might express their sexuality with adults, or specifically with and towards them. Ancient Greece would be cited, other cultures, other times, other places. In the 1970s, the UK Paedophile Information Exchange or PIE posited itself as a movement for sexual liberation, it cynically attempted to align itself with campaigners for gay rights: both groups were reviled on account of their sexuality. PIE produced button badges with 'Consent, not age' around the outside, with 'PIE' in the middle. I have no idea how many individuals actually wore one, or if anyone observing knew what it meant. The sense, in 2022, is that elements of this movement have returned, 'minor attracted persons' or 'MAPs' have emerged online, sometimes supported by academics, to suggest that it is stigma and rejection that makes it more likely for them to offend, or more properly not seek help.

One man I dealt with who was the cryptographer of a discovered conspiracy of CSEM disseminators, would write pages and pages of justifications for his interests and conduct, a manifesto of sorts. He would present it to me as an explanation of his offending. It was full of autobiographical accounts of his own childhood experiences, his suggestions as to how children might be liberated from societal constraints; it often lurched into the pornographic and the nauseating. I had to ask him to write less, to offer less, the opposite of my default position, for fear of becoming contaminated. He was, as many of the early offenders were, highly technically accomplished but socially inept, a stereotype, an isolate. It was easy to view him, and the other men like him, as deviant outliers, a special category of offender whom the authorities might, with technical skill and dedication, eventually suppress.

By 2005, probably earlier, it was clear, and I suspect it was inevitable given the forces at work on the Internet, that these almost comfortable stereotypes had been superseded by a mass of what the Detective calls 'ordinary men.' I was confronted and challenged by their essential mundanity. A number had clear learning difficulties, or evidenced autism. Many were as 'blokeish' as could be imagined, they ran football clubs in their spare time. Many were professionals, in highly paid and highly regarded employment. They included an anaesthetist who had been honoured by his profession, a 'rocket scientist' (such men exist), a cruise ship captain, various surveyors, bankers, accountants, police officers, and teachers.

Because of the nature of my role, almost all were fathers: I would be charged with conducting a risk assessment to ascertain if it would be safe for them to return home, or if they needed to be removed from home, or be denied or allowed contact with their children. I would agonise over my conclusions. Some had been divorced in rancorous circumstances, others remained in a marriage characterised by constraint and uncertainty. A number were not allowed to sleep in the same house as their children, although they might visit in the day and stay for as long as they wished: like vampires, their dangerousness was only considered potent or extant at night. One slept in his car on the driveway, one slept in the garage attached to the house and would wordlessly emerge through a connecting door into the kitchen at breakfast. One slept in a tent in the back garden, his little children thought it was novel, he was on holiday every day. All expressed a weary and cynical acceptance of their own powerlessness and whether with stoicism or not, had to manage the uncertainty as to when matters might be resolved.

For some years I assisted in running groups through which men on bail, awaiting sentence, might receive 'psycho-education' and a degree of support. The spectre of suicide often loomed: many had thought about it, some had attempted it, it was an irrational solution to a problem created by irrationality. The groups were run in the evening, usually in a church or Quaker meeting room. My co-worker and I would, on the first evening, try to predict who from the throng of men approaching the building would be attending. We were usually wrong. Many passed the door a few times, trying not to be early, trying not to stand out, bracing themselves. The group would usually represent the first time they discussed or acknowledged their conduct: they were required to own it. The first question asked of them, at least if I were running the agenda, would be 'What did you think you were doing?' It inevitably provoked ten sighs, ten sets of shrugged shoulders, a few stuttered replies. By week ten there would be some insight, some acceptance, a lessening of denial in most cases, an improvement in empathy. Of the ten men in attendance, there would always be one, sometimes two, where I sensed something else was at work in them; that they attended, not for insight or even for comfort, but as a means of appearing to be addressing their own faults whilst actually constructing a smokescreen through which to avoid censure and consequence.

I hope the reader is as exasperated by Geoff as I wanted them to be. I did not want him to be perfectly penitent and insightful; early on most men in his position are not. Most men focus on the immediacy of their own losses and shame, they struggle to connect their conduct as downloaders with the suffering of unknown others. They blame the Internet, talk about 'child pornography', resent their own arrest in the certain knowledge that thousands of others go unpunished. Geoff's suicide allows him to pass on the consequences of his behaviour to his wife and children, and to those who have to deal with his decision: the train driver, whoever gets to remove his body from the railway tracks, the Detective. He is not a bad man in reality, although he does bad things, just as Diana is a good person, but bad things happen to her. In 'The Daughter' I decided to show Geoff as a loving and dedicated father, I wanted there to be no ambiguity about that. He harms children at one remove: as the Detective tells him, he has dirty hands. If he lived, he may well have come to understand and accept that.

The question for most people engaging with Geoff's story who are not engaged in work with men like him is, I assume: how is his behaviour to be understood? As I have expressed elsewhere, the 'typical' downloader does not exist, he is characterised by diversity. Some consumers of the material, be it photographs, video, or fantasy stories are ego syntonic: they view and read in a state of unambiguous pleasure. For men with an unambiguous sexual interest in children with a history of sexual offending, whether discovered or not, the material is a constant source of joy and interest. Our assumptions that all viewers consume in that way are false: some men view in a state of ambivalence, anxiety, horror, pleasure, guilt, lust, nausea, and shame: they are ego dystonic.

Geoff describes a slippery slope. That slope exists. 'Mainstream' pornography sites do, in fact, offer a suite of material that is not too far away from the unambiguously exploitative material Geoff migrates towards. Notions of incest or implied incest are commonplace, violence against women is archetypal, voyeurism, 'teens', exploitation, revenge, and trickery as precursors to sex are the staple of many sites. Controversies rage as to what proportion of material uploaded by 'amateurs' is uploaded without the consent of those portrayed in it. Algorithms exist, as sophisticated as any in the online world, that engage the viewer and nudge him towards pay sites. They keep him engaged and hungry.

The science underpinning the algorithms that maintain engagement on legal pay sites is becoming known, and the psychological impulses which underpin the self-driven shift towards abusive content are emerging, albeit they remain controversial. Although most intuitive explanations of CSEM viewing appear to be based on the viewer's lust and sexual ambition, the reality may be more nuanced. There is, I think, significant resistance to considering drivers which appear to let men off the hook of culpability. These explanations are not, in my view, excuses: if we are to prevent recidivism and engage men on the cusp of offending and divert them into treatment we must help them understand behaviours which, for many, are genuinely puzzling and distressing.

The connection between an arresting sexual image, arousal and the creation of non sexual impulsivity is well established. Advertisers, at least in the West, have connected the half dressed woman with products that have nothing to do with sex for as long as advertising has existed. Why are Formula One racing drivers shielded from the sun at the start line by beautiful women holding umbrellas? Why do casinos favour attractive croupiers? Why is a buxom woman bending over in high heels and in her underwear taking a chicken out of an oven used to sell deodorant? 'Can she make you lose control?' was the by-line.

Many of the men I have dealt with as downloaders, over two decades, express what seems to be genuine puzzlement at their own conduct. They see themselves as normal men, not 'sex offenders' or 'paedophiles.' Most have no knowledge of the impact of pornography on their decision making, their desires and their choices: they do not read text books or study scientific journals. I have taken to setting out three suggested 'psychological drivers' for men in that state of ignorance. In most, if not all cases, the exposition leads to unconscious head nodding, or an explicit recognition of the reality of the experience.

What is termed 'The bikini effect' suggests that men in a state of even mild sexual arousal or awareness, however that has been arrived at, are prone to prefer short term gain and pleasure over a consideration of long term consequence. In the extreme, their empathy is reduced. Pornography offers no feedback or check, it encourages greedy and amoral consumption. The regular viewer's choices begin to incorporate the forbidden, the dark, the nihilistic, and the taboo.

Many men find their palate becomes jaded with what they have already seen and engaged with: they seek novelty and variety because habituation, the repeated viewing of the same thing, reduces their arousal and engagement. This latter phenomena, termed 'the Coolidge effect', leads to increasingly imaginative, and later increasingly deviant preoccupation: men 'chase' the highs of unambiguous, undifferentiated and unconstrained sexual pleasure. They become driven by forces and phenomena they are barely aware of.

Also connected to this migration is a form of episodic reinforcement that casinos utilise to keep the gambler engaged: occasional and random wins reinforce the behaviour, the prospect of the jackpot moves over the horizon. Many of the men I engage with describe this phenomena without knowing it has an identity: 'the slot machine effect.' They search and engage online because they hope to find something better than what they have already seen, to find something like it, but somehow different. They have a vague notion that somewhere, out there, will be the perfect image. Many refer to 'the holy grail' without choking on the words.

I imagined that Geoff was affected by these phenomena without, as is typical, being aware of them. He lacks insight, and his description of episodic feelings of pleasure, 'the ape in me' as he describes it, being balanced by or in conflict with his anxieties probably describes three quarters of the men I have dealt with. His shame, on discovery, is most painfully attached to his wife, but he is also concerned, as if in an unfunny situation comedy, with what the neighbours might think. He discovers, without surprise, that they think badly of him. They spray 'paedo' on his garage door.

Geoff's experience of social workers is, again, typical. He resents their assumptions that he poses a risk to his children without being able to appreciate how it must look to them. They do not engage him as much as they engage his wife, she alone experiences their scepticism and judgement. His contact with the children is fraught, meaningless, spoilt by the artificiality of the context. What might have been fun in the past, the family game, becomes a penance for him.

I remember that after the first performance of 'The Wife', one observer questioned the necessity of Geoff's suicide, they felt he was dead already, as both a father and a husband: he would not be able to meaningfully engage in either role again. I felt it a fair point, but defended it on the basis that it provided a full stop to the piece, cemented Diana's despair, and reflected some realities. My shallow explanation for the suicides of men who are under investigation for downloading is that they are killed by shame. I suspect that their own and probably sincere view of themselves is that they do not pose a risk to their children, they are not paedophiles, they are not irredeemable. They believe, however, that that is exactly how they are perceived. On that basis, the difference between the how they perceive themselves and how they know others see them is so out of kilter, so dissonant, that self destruction appears to provide a solution.

I have lost count of the number of men who have told me that suicide had crossed their minds, or that they had ruminated on it in the period between their arrest and their being sentenced. I have also lost count of the number of police officers who have told me about suspects or offenders they had dealt with who had taken their own lives. Some did so spectacularly, one by driving a car into a tree, most did so quietly, being found dead in their bedsit, completely isolated and broken.

I had a tangential connection with an individual who laid on a railway track after having left a note for the train driver. I cannot, forty odd years on, fathom whether it was an act of empathy, or one of self indulgence. I suspect he was too young to have thought it through at all. Ultimately, I felt that Geoff's act was one of escape for him, but it was not selfless. He leaves his wife with hundreds of unanswered questions, and his children with a double stigma. Inadvertently, and unknowingly, his act pushes the Detective over an edge he has been skirting for months.

The Daughter

The daughter is seventeen, white. Gentle, pale, unobtrusive. She veers between fragile and hardened, confident and child like. She's wearing a tracksuit, a can of Monster, or similar gaudy energy drink is in her hand. She swigs from it from time to time.

My dad died when I was nine. [*Looks away, looks back, looks away, pause, looks back.*]

When I tell people that they look surprised and sorry. I'm seventeen now and I must have told this story a hundred times. I can usually see them, the people I tell, or have to tell, struggling about what to say next. 'Oh . . . I'm sorry' is usually it. I get 'Oh God, that's awful, sorry' sometimes. There's usually a pause then, as they think of the next words: 'Was he ill? Was it an accident?' are what usually comes next, if anything comes at all.

For the first three or four years I used to dread people asking, now I almost look forward to the confusion, see them struggling. I manage my face to give nothing away, like a Sphynx my gran used to say. It took me years before I could spell Sphynx and once I could I looked it up on Google. I knew what she meant then. I am a Sphynx now, there's nothing you can see, but underneath the stone face there's a lot going on, a lot of feeling, a lot of bleeding, in the past, sometimes literally. [*Unconsciously smooths hand over forearm.*]

Anyway, my dad died when I was nine. He was on bail for

possession of indecent imagery and he killed himself. He stepped in front of a train. He killed himself. That's what I tell people now.

It's been eight years. A lot's gone on, like. What can I remember? There's two childhoods I had, before and after. Not quite before and after his death, but before and after the police came, that was like the point where my childhood died.

My mum doesn't know this, I've never told her, but I was awake when they came, when the police came. I didn't know who it was, of course, but my brother came into my room, it was still dark, and he said there were a lot of people downstairs, talking. For some reason we both knew we couldn't go down there, I could hear my dad talking in a voice he didn't use at home, he sounded nervous, like he never sounded before. I used to think he was invincible. We both stood at the top of the stairs, me and my brother, barely breathing, and when my dad started up the stairs with another man we just ducked into our bedrooms and stayed there until they'd gone. I didn't even notice they'd taken him with them. He just . . . disappeared.

We had a year where, I can hardly remember this, but my brother can, my dad used to come round and visit us, erm, have contact with us, whilst my mum was there. We used to sit and play games, but I just have this one memory of it, just the one incident. We were playing Buckaroo, with the donkey thing that kicks all the objects off its back. It was my dad's from when he was child, he'd just kept it, all the pieces were there. It used to be fun, the legs kicking up, the stuff on its back going everywhere, me and my brother and my mum and dad cheering. It didn't matter who won.

This one time, the last time we played it, Buckaroo, the time I remember, it went off, the donkey, the donkey kicked and it all went flying, and we all just sat there, in silence. [*Counts off, on her fingers*]: The blanket, the saddle, the shovel, the canteen, the pan, the lantern, the bedroll, the rope, the dynamite, the hat, the holster, the guitar, and the crate, they all flew off. See, I told you I could remember.

I was only nine but I could feel the wrongness of it, the weirdness; the anger in my mum's face, I couldn't explain that, the sadness in my dad's face. [*Pause.*] I couldn't understand it, but it was there. This horrible tension. My mum just picked up all the things off the table and the floor, and the donkey, silently, and put the whole lot back in the box. After my dad died, I saw it in the bin, my mum just put the whole box in the black bin, didn't even separate it out for recycling. That wasn't like her, but she got even less like her later.

I did save something from the bin. Well, not the bin exactly, but it felt like it. About a month after my dad died my mum sorted all his things out, mostly for the charity shop. They were all in the hall in these big shopping bags, bags for life, she was always buying them as she'd always forget to take the ones she already owned to the shops with her. It was a running joke, she might come back from the shops with a couple of new ones and my dad would go 'Makes a change! Bags for life! I'll be a hundred before we get through them all!' [*Pause, exhales noisily, settles self.*]

Anyway, there were maybe a dozen bags, my eye was drawn to one of them, right at the top of it, folded up, it was my dad's dressing gown. It was this big fluffy thing, dark blue, like really dark. It had this massive picture of Homer Simpson on the front, he's holding a can of that beer he drinks, and he's smiling, with his thumb up by the side of his face. I don't remember getting it for him, I was too young, but he always told me it was his favourite present, and that me and my brother bought it for him.

When I was little, I think I'd just started school, I had these nightmares, where I was in bed, and it felt like the bedroom was a universe, massive, the door was a million million miles away, the window a million million miles away, and my bed was this refuge, but it was like a raft that was sinking. I'd be half awake, half asleep, and I remember calling out, crying, for someone to cross this void, the void between the bed and the door, and come and rescue me. It was always my dad. The door would swing open and he'd cross the space in an instant, it was only three or four feet really, and he'd pull me out of bed and sit me on his knee. He'd be wearing his dressing gown, of course, and my head would rest against his chest, I could hear his heart beating, slow. My face would be resting against the material, the bright yellow of Homer's head. The smell, too, it was some sort of clean smell, like shower gel or aftershave or something. Not that nasty teenage boy smell, sweat, Lynx, whatever, but something grown up and dark, powerful. I'd just nestle into it, feel the softness of it, hear my dad's heart beating, hear him talking, telling me stories about things, just the sound of his voice, and I'd drift off to sleep and wouldn't wake until morning, and I'd be in my bed and the door was only feet away and the window was only feet away, and everything was safe.

Anyway, like I said, my mum was throwing it out, my dad's dressing gown, giving it away, to strangers. I pulled it out of there and put it in my bedroom, hid it in my cupboard. She'd washed it, so it smelt like all my clothes instead of like him, and I sort of hated her for doing that, but she didn't know what it meant to me. At night, I'd get it out, once I'd pretended to go to sleep, and I used it like a blanket, or a sheet really, I'd lie on it, rest my face on it, try to remember his heart beat, the smell of shower gel and aftershave. After a few weeks my mum found out, came into my room to check on me, and I was lying on it. Next thing I knew she'd pulled me out of bed, she was crying, wailing, it was a bit frightening, and she wrapped us up in it, was rocking from side to side, sitting on the bed, with me on her knee and the dressing gown wrapped round us both. She didn't really say anything, once she'd stopped crying she just put me back into bed and covered me up with it, sort of smoothed my hair down and walked out. We never discussed it; I just kept it, but I stopped hiding it.

My brother, he took it in the way that boys do. He battered others, or tried to, whilst I battered myself, kind of. Kids at school took to calling him 'paedo', or 'son of paedo', 'son of dead paedo' if they were really going for him, because it was all in the papers before my dad died. He'd be just walking down the corridor, or getting off the bus, and it'd be like a chorus, he'd just try to pretend they weren't shouting it at him, but it was pretty obvious, everyone looked at him, see what his reaction was. Most times he'd manage to ignore it, but not others.

My grandad had this Johnny Cash album, vinyl, all scratchy, and I remember when we used to go round there, before and after our dad died, and he'd put it on. Not that we asked him to. There's this song 'A Boy Named Sue', it's about a man who abandons his son but calls him Sue before he leaves, to make him tough, or so he says. Anyway, there's a line in it 'Some girl would giggle and he'd get red, some boy would laugh and he'd bust his head.' That was my brother, he was always in fights, he'd lose most of the time as he's not that big, but he'd give it a go, and half the time he'd get excluded for a couple of days just to, like, rub it in.

The other thing was, he looked like my dad, same hair and everything. When he was little people used to point it out, 'like he was Mini Me', as my dad said, I only understood what that meant later too. He used to lean back in his chair the way our dad did, or do that thing where he'd put his hands together, like in prayer, when he was thinking, all sorts of things, as well as his hair. But once our dad was dead, and my mum might say, absent minded like, that he was 'just like his dad' [makes quote marks], then it'd go quiet, she'd look embarrassed, there'd be this long silence, like the Buckaroo silence, you know. It got so that we never really mentioned it, just look forward, not back. That was the message we gave ourselves.

My mum changed. Before my dad died, well before the police came, she was fun, always acting like there was nothing in the world to be worried about, like she could manage anything. After, she sort of shrank away a bit. People were so cruel, the neighbours just wouldn't meet her eye, the graffiti that appeared on the garage door made her paranoid, she thought it was one of them, we never found out. She did all the things she was supposed to, you know? Cook and that, helped us with our homework, took us on holiday, organised stuff like Christmas and birthdays. It took me a couple of years to realise she was going through the motions, her smile was fake, she was . . . [*pauses for the words*] hollowed out? Do you know what I mean? There was this odd way about her, loads of things we couldn't talk about, share. For a bit I really hated her, I thought if she'd tried harder, been nicer to my dad then he might not have done it, done what he did. For a bit after that I really hated him, for leaving us, for not taking whatever was coming to him.

Partly because I couldn't talk to my mum, and partly because I was thirteen or fourteen and almost all the girls I was at school with were doing it, I used to go on these sites, websites, suicide sites, to see if I could work out why he'd done it, or at least . . . well I don't really know why I was there, or what I wanted. [*Pause, takes a breath.*] I wanted him back, that's what I wanted. Anyway, I didn't find any answers, just a lot of other desperate people, loads of girls, I guess they were girls, said they were girls anyway. There was always someone thinking about doing it, or saying they'd attempted it, and I'd be there, offering advice, like I knew anything worth listening to! [*Laughs.*]

On these sites. It got dark. Well, it started pretty dark and it got darker. After a bit there'd be these other chats and streams, about cutting, self harm, you know? Once I tried it, it seemed like a solution, the pain would take my pain away. The blood carried it away. I'd feel like I could choose when I felt pain, instead of having it shoved down my throat. My mum would plead with me to stop doing it, I had a counsellor at school, I had that CAMHS, I had a group, I had pills, I had my brother shouting at me, I had all sorts. Despite all that the scars built up, scar on scar, the pain on the pain. It got . . . close.

In the end, it was my aunt. Gemma. She was married to my mum's brother, he was in the police, I didn't really trust him, because of that maybe, I don't know. He was alright though. But my Aunt Gemma, she was close enough to know all about it, but not close enough to have been really hurt by it. This one time, she came round, took me out for a walk, in the park. It felt pretty lame. Boring. Pointless, at least to start with.

She said a couple of things that made sense. One was that it wasn't my fault: in all the years since he died no one had said that, no one had thought to say it because it was so obvious, but it needed saying, I'd been thinking it was . . . my . . . fault. Because I was nine, and when you're nine you think everything's about you, don't you? The second thing was how proud she was of me, for sticking it out, for just, still being here, and for not, well, you know [*embarrassed*] going through with anything. She'd no kids of her own, but she said she'd always looked on me, from a distance, as a daughter she'd have liked to have.

It wasn't what she said, exactly, it was more that she was bothered, after all the trouble I'd brought she was still there, just there, to walk round this stupid park with this stupid scared and scarred girl, and feed the stupid ducks, like I was five, and just sit. We just sat. Silent. My eyes burned but I wouldn't cry.

It started getting dark, so we walked home and she held my hand, I let her because it was dark and no one would see, but I wanted her to. We got home and my mum was sitting in the chair she always sat in, looking at the piano, sort of, and I rushed over to her and I bent down and I hugged her so hard, pulled into her and I told her I loved her and I was sorry and I missed my dad sooo much. She hugged me back and said she loved me back, and then we cried about it, and him, for probably the last time.

I still miss him, and I love him. And I still love her.

Notes on 'The Daughter'

The daughter was the last of the monologues to be written, and its creation came from some correspondence and discussion I had with a charity, 'Children Heard and Seen', who I had engaged with on social media. The charity works with children who have a parent in prison, and provides one-to-one support and other services to help children make sense of their circumstances and foster a greater sense of self, sense of purpose, and sense of belonging. There is no statutory responsibility on anyone to offer these children a service or support, and I sense that their neglect by the state and society might be viewed as part of the punishment meted out to the parent. There is something ancient, and literally Biblical about this notion, along the lines of the sins of the father being visited upon the children.

I was asked, by Children Seen and Heard, if I could apply myself to the experience of a child whose father was imprisoned, but determined that it might be as useful, in terms of dealing with the issues and in completing the circle of connections I had in mind in *Crossing the Line*, to consider how Geoff's son and daughter might be affected by their father's plight. Save for his death, the dynamic features were the same, his absence from their lives permanent rather than temporary.

The experience of children whose father is suspected of having viewed child abuse material are, of course, affected by perceptions of risk. I would never claim to be an advocate of Donald Trump's strategies, but his cynical and seductive description of the potential risks posed by Mexican migrants bears consideration here: 'If I had a bowl of one hundred sweets, and one or two of them were poisoned, would you let me offer them to your children?' Of course, it is possible that all one hundred Mexican migrants might be entirely benign, but Trump's world view does not allow for that. The genuine problem men like Geoff pose to Children's Services is, of course, how they might differentiate men who offer a direct sexual risk to their own children from men who do not. Diana's resentment at Children's Services is based, in part, upon the clumsy way in which they raise the matter, and in part, upon her own instinctive denial. The simple cognitive dissonance: 'Nice men don't abuse children. —— is a nice man. —— wouldn't abuse children' is commonplace.

In the early years of arrests of downloaders, my sense was that the police had a genuine belief they were rescuing the children present in the household. Now, I sense their ambivalence: for every 'old school child molester' they find, they describe unearthing a number of nihilistic pornography users, some men with autistic traits, a number of potential suicides and some individuals who simply baffle them. They are prosecuted just the same: the offence is an absolute one and the police have the luxury of not having to prove or discern a motive. Social workers inhabit a world characterised by the grey shades of risk, but they have to make black and white decisions: should a father stay in the household or not? Can he have contact with his children or not? Should the Local Authority issue legal proceedings or not?

My own mental construction of Geoff was that he had not abused his children and that he was not going to, but the reader of the monologues cannot know that. Nor, in any non-fictional case of revealed downloading, can any social worker. Almost all of the men I have engaged are quick to point out that whatever they have viewed, for however long, has not had an impact upon their views of their children or their ambitions towards them. I was, in one of the earliest showings of 'The Wife', rather taken aback to have one of the social work participants suggest that the reason Geoff's children failed to buy or wrap his dressing gown might be because they resented him, maybe he had abused them without their mother knowing. Such things are possible, and I wondered if I was defending my fictional Geoff too enthusiastically.

Police operations against downloaders are routine now, some 850 men are arrested every month, with ten families per day experiencing what Diana and her son and daughter experience. Operations that target a group of offenders are often announced with the suggestion that 'Eighty-three men have been arrested and one hundred and thirty children have been safeguarded', but the notion of 'safeguarding' remains stubbornly vague. The implication is that the children have been rescued from sexual abuse, or the prospect of it. What is not mentioned, because it is generally left unaddressed, is how the children are safeguarded from the negative effects of the necessary police and state involvement. Women in Diana's position, and police officers like the Detective all use the same language: 'the Knock' is akin to a grenade being deployed in a family home, regardless of what else follows. I recently heard a woman describe how, as the police left her home, taking her husband with them, one of the detectives mouthed 'sorry', silently, as he backed out of the door.

The daughter's experience, and her brother's experience as she describes them are commonplace. She loves her father and misses him. Her descriptions of childhood nightmares were essentially my own. I was born just months before the Cuban missile crisis, and something of that, or of the threat of nuclear annihilation that followed it for over a decade may have been in the air when I was a child, the BBC television news was a family staple and I may have absorbed the sense of impotence and threat in the face of that by a sort of aural osmosis. At three or four years of age, if I awoke at night, the window in my bedroom would, as the daughter describes, appear to be a universe away. My dad would lift me out of my bed during my own nightmarish screaming and carry me downstairs, to sit on his lap until I fell asleep. I recall being comforted and a little awed by his strength.

For the daughter, as well as for Diana, Geoff's death means most of the mysteries of his behaviour will never be resolved. The daughter cannot understand his enforced absence, although she knows something is wrong, and sucks up the tension in the household like a sponge. After her father's death, she finds a dangerous form of relief in self harm. Self harm is remarkably common in adolescent girls, and sites which purport to offer support in relation to it are frequently places that celebrate and revel in it. The vulnerability of the daughter is akin to the vulnerability of girls, and boys, who are approached online for sexual purposes: the Internet is an ungoverned space, it ought not be an environment where children roam unattended, but it is difficult to conceive, now, how that stable door might now be bolted.

Boys whose fathers are convicted of sexual offences are at particular risk of being associated with their father's conduct, as if the tendency were genetic, hence sudden anxieties about 'being just like his father.' Gender identity is, of course, central to how a boy might view himself in relation to a father charged with sexual offences, and my imagined sense of Geoff's son was that he would attempt to reassert his challenged masculinity through violence.

One lens through which these secondary traumas for children might be measured is in relation to a body of theory relating to adverse childhood experiences or ACEs. This suggests that the most commonly discerned and documented harmful life events a child might experience, in combination, lead to a significant reduction in long term health and life chances. In terms, the thesis is that abuse leads to stress, and in childhood abuses cannot, for the most part, be escaped from: the neglected child or the sexually abused child are rarely identified and removed from the environment that harms them. Interventions are rare. Children subject to such experience live, therefore, with a constant sense of threat and anxiety: their adrenaline levels at a constant peak, their internal alarm constantly ringing. As adolescence approaches, and children have greater freedom and agency, they may seek to manage or forget their experiences by resorting to behaviours that bring temporary relief. Alcohol and drugs are diverting and fun, but they are dangerous too. Self harm, in terms of cutting, provides diversion and a physical expression of something that words cannot describe. Sexual adventures may provide temporary esteem or diversion, but they may lead to rape, exploitation or an ultimately diminished sense of self.

Of course, children who engage in drug taking, alcohol, or various 'adventures' do not tend to prosper in school: they are marginalised, excluded and discounted. School leavers without qualifications may fail to find employment, they experience higher levels of poverty, their self esteem is compromised, and they are at greater risk of involvement in crime. Crime leads to imprisonment, imprisonment leads to further alienation, homelessness, depression, addictions and a spiralling sense of worthlessness. That sense is managed by further use of narcotics or alcohol; rage leads to violence, injury, debility, and in the classic and brutal exposition of the ACEs, early death. In crude but inexorable actuarial terms: the more ACEs a child experiences, the shorter their life expectation; the emotional and moral injury of trauma essentially wear out the body.

There are ten childhood experiences that the ACE model considers.

They are not weighted: sexual abuse is counted a one, parental divorce or separation as another, although I would imagine that a sexually abused child might suffer more trauma than one whose parents separate amicably. Setting that aside, it is profoundly concerning that so many of the adverse events set out in the ACE feature, or may feature, as consequences of the father's online conduct and as consequences of the discovery of that conduct. Emotional abuse or emotional neglect may precede the discovery, since the father may be preoccupied by his behaviour and emotionally distant or absent. Post discovery, many children suffer the agonies of stigma that attaches to all sexual offenders and to many children whose parents are imprisoned. Women who are traumatised by the experience of dealing with consequences that are not of their making may be emotionally unavailable to their children for months. Some of the men I deal with describe abusing alcohol or drugs in parallel with their online conduct, they may resort to the same as a means of dealing with their arrest: so might their partners. Mental ill health is well documented now as being a consequence of 'the Knock', as mothers and partners struggle to manage the enormity of their situation. Parental separation or divorce are likely, separation is almost inevitable in the short term. Parental imprisonment is a possibility, and children whose parents are imprisoned for sexual offences appear, sadly, to be multiply stigmatised.

Thus, seven of the ten delineated ACEs appear to attach, at least potentially, to an episode of downloading and its discovery. The presence of six ACEs is said to reduce life expectancy by 20 years. The question for the state, and those employed by the state, is: 'What steps might we take to reduce the consequences of our own intervention?' I am not suggesting, of course, that the state do nothing about CSEM viewing, those who cannot be diverted or deterred from it need to be identified and held to account. It

must be the case, however, that protective steps and interventions
be offered at the same time as the criminal enquiry takes its course.
We know, now, what the consequences of our inevitable but planned
interventions in families are likely to be, and we need to plan for
and minimise them.

The question for individuals seeking to safeguard children
in circumstances where a parent has been found to have viewed
and downloaded child abuse material remains: what are they
safeguarding children from? The first concern must, of course,
be sexual abuse, be that something that has already occurred or
which might occur in the future. When the phrase 'One hundred
children were safeguarded' is used that is essentially what is meant:
the viewer has been arrested, and he is, one assumes, to be denied
unsupervised contact with his children.

Ultimately, 'safeguarding' is significantly more nuanced and
complex than 'child protection.' Some of long term harms that accrue
to children subject to state intervention may, in truth, be located
in the system's response to revealed, reported, or suspected abuses.
Children's needs, in UK systems, are regarded as 'paramount', but
this need not be used as a philosophy or weapon by which competent
parents' needs are bulldozed or disregarded, or the idea of their
being recruited to help their own children recover be discounted.
There are, of course, dangerous and incompetent parents, but I do
not think it utopian to suggest that most mothers know and love
their children more than the state can.

The Mother

The mother is in her mid forties. She is working class, and not obviously bright, but she bursts with pride about her child, and with indignation about what happens to her. Her articulacy comes from her fury. There is wisdom in what she says. She sits at a kitchen table, with tea pot and cup and saucer. In the background, perhaps hanging off a shelf or a dresser, are a selection of medals, on ribbons, the sort you get just for participating.

She was my pride and joy, my daughter. It wasn't easy, she wasn't expected, you know. Well, wasn't planned, that's a better way of putting it. I'd been married and divorced, he was the wrong sort. I realised that before we'd even married, but I couldn't back out, my dad had paid for the reception and the caterers, and there were too many people to let down, so I just grinned and beared it. For six years, mind, I don't give up easily. He wasn't abusive or anything, just not very bothered. In the end he just looked at me over the dinner table and said: 'I think we're done, don't you?' I knew exactly what he meant, I think he had someone else, but we parted as friends.

I went a bit wild after that, three boyfriends I had, [*emphasis, suggesting, in her own mind at least, she was a party girl*] in less than three years, I was nearly thirty years old by then, my mum said I'd be left on the shelf, that I'd missed the boat, that I could walk through the woods and still come out with a crooked stick.

Peter, her dad's name was. I worked in a dry cleaners and he used to come in with his suits. After a bit he'd start to chat, and then I realised he only had two suits and I was cleaning them every couple of weeks. We got to talking, and he asked me out, and well you know the rest . . . [*pause, eyes to heaven*]. My mum said, she was good for these phrases, my mum said that if two idiots went into a field, one of them would come out pregnant. Well that idiot was me, because as soon as I told him about it he told me it was a big mistake and that he was married, and that was that. My religion and my conscience wouldn't let anything else happen, so Leanne was born, on the first of April 1999. The only fool that day was me, but I did love her so.

It was always a struggle. I wasn't much for school, so I had no exams to speak of, and shop work doesn't pay much, but my mum and dad helped out a bit, and I worked on and off, and Leanne kind of made everything bright, like sunshine, she was my sunshine, brightened my day every day. [*Lights up.*] I'd sing that song to her, when she was little, and as she grew up she used to join in, [*sings*]: 'You are my sunshine, my only sunshine, you make me happy, when skies are grey.' I think my mum must have sung it to me, as it's an old song isn't it?

Anyway, Leanne wasn't much for school either, especially at seniors, and she didn't do that well, was slow on her reading, terrible at maths and that, I couldn't help much with the complicated stuff, although in the shop I could work out change in my head. She'd still got a bit of puppy fat, and the other kids used to tease her about that, and about her red hair, which I thought was her crowning glory and they said was ginger. But she could swim like a fish. I used to take her every Saturday, before she could even walk, and she took to it, like, I was going to say like a fish to water, [*shrugs, laughs*] but she did.

This one time at the swimming pool, they had a class in, these kids going up and down in lanes, and Leanne was in the pool, and she was going faster than the other kids, and I was cheering and pointing, and this man in a tracksuit came over and he said she should take it up properly, that Leanne had something special. He was the coach, like, and he seemed nice and that he knew what he was doing, so that was that, I signed her up.

After that it was swimming every weekend, and three mornings a week, up at six, in the pool by half past, out at half past eight in time for school. She was down for county trials, and she won at most distances: Juniors, under twelve champion, under thirteen champion, all that, me shouting from the side like a mad woman whilst everyone else seemed to be looking at their phones. Sean, the coach, he used to take her off for galas and that, with the other girls and boys in a van, and she used to come home with her eyes lit up with the excitement of it all. He'd pop in for a cup of tea sometimes, and there was a point where I thought he might be interested. My mum would tease me about it, but I just said he was like a brother I didn't have, and a father Leanne didn't have either. She still had no friends to speak of, but she was so happy, her bedpost had all these medals dangling from it, all these certificates on her wall, Sean said she could go to the nationals, and it made me proud. My Leanne, my sunshine.

I first started to feel something was up because of the phone I bought her. She had this old one my dad got her from a car boot, but she said it was a loser's phone, it just did text messages and that, wasn't like an iPhone or anything, like all her mates had, so I got her one for Christmas. Had to get one of those loans. You could do everything with it, the phone, apps and that, look on the Internet, take photos, you name it. After a bit she started to spend more and more of her time in her room, which I thought was a teenage thing, it's what I did at that age, but after a bit it didn't seem right, and I'd ask her if she was alright and she'd say she was; we'd have this sort of staring contest where I was trying to read her mind and she was trying to stop me, and I'd have to leave it there.

I was at work when I got a call. Nice man, kind voice, said he was a police detective, asked if I could come down to the station, Leanne was there and she was a bit upset and they wanted to talk to her about something and it would be best if I came down. On the way over there, on the bus, I was imagining all sorts, like she'd been truanting, shoplifting, or she'd been bullied, or, well I don't know what. The detective met me, and asked about Leanne's swimming, and if she'd been enjoying it, was she worried about it, or anything like that, because they'd had a complaint, not from Leanne, but from another girl, about their coach, Sean, and she'd said it had happened to Leanne too.

I said there must be a mistake, as Leanne told me everything, we were that close, and we had no secrets, but as soon as the words came out of my mouth I could see her face, in her bedroom, telling me she was alright, with her phone held behind her back, and suddenly I realised I knew nothing about her at all, and we'd become strangers somehow, and I'd failed her.

We went off to this little house, very clean it was like no one lived there, and no one did, it was this place where they interviewed children. I was in this side room with a social worker, and there were two TVs, one showing Leanne sitting there on a sofa, one showing the back of her head and the detective, leaning in like he expected to hear some secrets. Leanne was in the next room but it felt like she was miles away from me, she had this teddy on her knee, which looked all wrong as she'd given all her teddies away years before, now she looked like a tiny child, and the sunshine was gone from her. Before she said a word I knew what had happened, and I cried so much they had to warn me that it might put her off, she might hear it through the wall.

The story came out. [*Pause, sigh, pause.*] It had all started on those trips out, she was always last to get dropped off, and Sean used to brush her leg with his hand when he changed gear. She said she never said anything to him, and that she thought he might have done it by accident, but after a couple of times he sort of left his hand there and she couldn't think what to do. She'd never had a boyfriend, she was just thirteen and he must have been touching forty, and she said she was curious, and excited, and that she liked him.

I think she wanted a dad. Not that he was acting like a dad, God forbid. I'm getting all this wrong, mixed up, but she was flattered, like he gave her attention, praise, made her feel like she was something, 'sassy' she'd call it, when all her so called friends at school just kept saying she was stupid, and that she'd never be anything, that swimming was all she was good for and who wanted to do that anyway?

She said that after a few weeks he started to send her messages. The police had them all anyway, they'd taken his phone off him and they were all still on there. It started with the odd kiss, like a few x's, then those symbol things, lips kissing, thumbs up, hearts, all that. She'd be sending them back, he'd be saying she wasn't just another swimming student to him, she was important, and he'd sort of fallen for her, he couldn't help it. She'd be saying she loved him, and that she'd wait as long as it took, like they had a future. Then he started to ask for pictures, you know, of her . . . naked. [*Ashamed.*] And she sent them, said she knew a lot of the kids at school were doing it, it didn't seem like a big deal, but once she sent one he asked for more, and she got frightened, he was sort of pushing her and pushing her, and the tone changed and he was threatening and well, he took advantage.

What she didn't want to talk about was that he'd, he'd done sexual things to her too, in the van, and that he'd filmed it on his phone. This was after she'd sent the photos. She said by then she'd realised he didn't have any feelings for her and that he was just getting what he could, and that she hated him for it. But she couldn't tell as it was her fault as she'd led him on, because that's what he told her, and she believed it. She didn't tell the detective about it that first time, but like I said, they had his phone and it was all on there, and on his computer at home, and it turned out he was a member of this group, on the Internet, and they were all egging each other on and boasting about what they'd been doing, and who they'd done it to. The detective was really nice about it, kind I mean, he didn't judge, he just said this Sean was a skilled manipulator, [*pause*] 'skilled manipulator', that was the phrase they used in court. It was all in the papers.

What had happened was that this other girl, I didn't know her, Leanne didn't really know her either, this other girl, he'd been doing the same to her. She was thirteen too, he'd told her the same things, said she was special, she'd sent him the same photos, he'd made the same sort of films of her. He'd done the same thing to four or five other girls over the years, two of them from the grammar school, and none of them had said a word until this last girl. She'd had some lesson at school, one of those ones where they show them a video and say 'don't let this happen to you!' But it already had, and she broke down and cried, and they asked questions.

There wasn't really a trial, thank God, because I don't think Leanne would have gone into any witness box and answered any questions. The detective said they had him cold as he'd recorded everything he did and he'd shared it with his friends. Friends he'd never met, mind, they just sort of find each other, like birds of a feather. He got eight years, Sean did, and they banned him from teaching swimming.

Leanne thought it was her fault, that she was dirty, that her secret shame was public property now, that hundreds of men in Sean's group had seen her, and that thousands of men would see her soon enough, because once her pictures were out there, there was no getting them back. I know there's men use that sort of thing for their entertainment, and God forgive them, because I won't.

Child pornography they call it, like she was some sort of paid you know what. I'm sorry, but that's what I think they must think, but she's my daughter and she didn't do anything wrong. The fault was on his side, that Sean, and on the side of all those others who've looked at my daughter being abused and have taken God knows what pleasure from it. Dirty men.

I think Leanne sees it the way I see it now, that she were blameless like, but it's taken a while. She did this group, lovely people running it, did paintings and writing and that, and they put her straight. My sunshine came back. [*Smiles, sings 'You Are My Sunshine.' Fade.*]

Notes on 'The Mother'

I wanted, through the mother's account, to offer a single, human insight into the forces at work when children are sexually abused, and how the trauma of that abuse is amplified by it being recorded and shared for the 'entertainment' of others, as the mother describes. In the main, prior to the growth of the Internet and the existence of the digital and mobile phone camera, children who were sexually abused experienced that abuse in secret and in isolation. In the pre-digital age, the fact of the abuse would only be known to the perpetrator and the child, unless the child chose to disclose. Children may be prevented from disclosing because they fear or love the perpetrator; because they are made to feel ashamed of something they have no real control over, or because they have been recruited to share the perpetrator's world view: that they 'led him on' or 'asked for it.'

It is small comfort, but most children abused prior to the growth of digital CSAM might retain an atom of control over their experience becoming known to others: if they did not want it known about, they might make that choice, however limited it might appear. They might tell a friend, a parent, or a counsellor, they might set out their experience to a police officer, like the detective. Their abuser would not, of course, boast about his conduct in public, or share photographs of it with others, say, in the local public house.

The digital age, and the incessant demand for new images of sexual abuse, for novelty, for variety, and for increasingly sadistic and unambiguously harmful content, has placed children at significant risk: both of abuse itself, and of that abuse being broadcast to countless consumers. Some children have, without their consent, of course, become famous in the depraved circles some viewers inhabit; their names, or 'series', become ubiquitous. Their abuser receives kudos and acclaim rather than condemnation. Viewers on darknet message boards eagerly await new images, or try to complete a series, like monstrous cigarette card or Pokémon collectors. Some children's names are attached to dates, as they grow, so that one might see, say, 'Alice 9', 'Alice 10', 'Alice 11', 'Alice 12', as the child ages and their abuser demonstrates his ongoing control over and access to her.

The child in these images may, of course, become conscious that their sufferings and humiliation have been broadcast to thousands or tens of thousands of strangers. What was once a private (but unwarranted) shame becomes a public one, and one that cannot be escaped from. Some charities working with children who have been the subjects of abuse captured on film describe those children, in adolescence or adulthood, as being haunted by the fear that any man they might pass on the street might recognise them. Suggestions are that exactly that fear has been realised by some.

Men I have worked with who are what we occasionally call 'simple downloaders', those who view imagery and do not produce it, often fail to acknowledge that they are dealing with images of real children. That may be because they simply cannot afford to: the pleasure they might derive would be lessened, or spoiled, if they were to attach the image and the activity to a real person. It may be that distance lends disinterest: the child in the picture is not like any child they know; he or she may be 'foreign', or 'different.'

Family men I see are always asked the same questions, by me, in assessments. The question 'what if you came across a photograph of your own children?', tends to produce promises of violence or death to the abuser. A particularly stubborn and unimaginative client was given a multiple choice quiz as to what he might do if he were to look out of his back bedroom window and see the next door neighbour sexually abusing his daughter in the garden: '(A) call the police; (B) go next door and save her; or (C) take photographs.' His reply: 'But I don't even know the people next door' did not offer much confidence that any empathic powers were in place. Distance, be it geographic, or racial, or simply the space between the viewer's eyes and the screen, seems to reduce concern.

Another tack might be to ask a man who had taken an interest in a 'series' what he imagined that child's hobbies or interests to be. Did they own a pet? What did they like to do at school? What did they want to do when they grew up? The discomfort was often palpable, the confusion real: many viewers of abusive imagery only tend to see the child as an object, as flesh, as a performer, or as a blank canvas for their sexual imaginings. The realisation that a child whose abuse they may have enjoyed, or found a distraction is a real person, with a hinterland, a real personality, three dimensions, and a right to dignity is a painful but necessary one.

The mother has something in common with the wife, of course. They are each connected, without knowing it, to both Geoff and to the Detective. Geoff, through his viewing CSAM, plunges his wife into a crisis that destroys her faith in him, and puts her own children at risk. He is also, albeit by implication, a consumer of the material Leanne's abuser, Sean, produces. Geoff has, as the Detective suggests, got dirty hands.

I wanted the detective to treat Diana humanely, most police officers of my personal and professional acquaintance do so. He visits her when he has no real duty to do so, she assaults him without him blaming her, or retaliating. By the same token, his dealings with the mother are professional and compassionate, he coaxes Leanne's disclosure from her, he treats the mother respectfully.

The mother is also, in the bureaucratic process adopted by Children's Services, likely to be regarded as 'a protective factor' in Leanne's life, just as Diana's capacity as the same in relation to her own children is actively and sceptically challenged. I cannot recall when that particularly cold and mechanistic phrase entered the social work argot: I think women in Diana's and the mother's shoes might prefer to be regarded a women, as mothers, and as persons in their own right rather than as 'factors', protective or otherwise, that the authorities might weigh in the balance.

The mother cannot be blamed for Leanne's experience, of course. The blame rests with Sean, just as in Diana's case it rests with Geoff, but I have been asked to assess many women like the mother once their children have been abused, in order to ascertain if they lack 'awareness' or 'protective skills.' Greater thought seems to be given to how protective women might be rather than to how dangerous men might be: the implication is that men cannot take responsibility or change and that women need to police them.

I wanted, through her speech, and through the initial description, to show that the mother had some intellectual limitations, but that her instincts and intentions were perfectly sound; that she was fierce. engaged and loving. Too many of my clients risk being written off as parents because they do not hit an arbitrary intellectual mark, or are seen as 'limited.' I sense, occasionally, that psychologists measure what can be measured, to lend apparent scientific rigour, when no such thing exists in relation to the human heart or parental competence. One woman I assessed had been previously adjudged as needing to have special measures in place for any formal court proceedings, yet her speech was rich in beautiful metaphor. She felt as if, in relation to her situation, she were 'on a fairground roundabout, going faster and faster, then a bulldozer hits it, and everything goes flying.' When her speech was quoted in my report, the suggestion from the Local Authority's barrister was that she may have employed a doppelgänger to undertake the interview.

The main purposes of 'The Mother', from a training or consciousness raising point of view, were to connect a real child to the notion of 'images', and to describe the process of grooming. 'Digital grooming' relates to the engagement of children in the online world. My experience is that the process of online grooming is significantly easier that what went before it: online offenders inhabit an environment devoid of impediment and laden with opportunity. Leanne's experience is different, a hybrid that begins in the offline world, with Sean using tried and tested approaches that utilise whatever is available to him. He 'inadvertently' brushes her leg whilst changing gear in the minibus, testing the water. He straddles the offline and online worlds, and provides images and, presumably, pornographic accounts of his dealings to men such as Geoff. He uses Leanne for his own gratification, but also for the secondary purpose of receiving kudos from men in his group 'who use that sort of thing for their entertainment', as the mother puts it.

There are some special features at work here, in terms of Leanne's relationship with her abuser. He is her coach, and sports coaching has been revealed, like the church, as an environment where abusers have operated with some confidence. Parents with ambitions for their children might vest the coach with special virtues, as they might invest a priest; both professions hint at opportunity, be that spiritual or occupational. Children view the coach, as they might view the priest, as benign and omnipotent. The church, and sporting institutions guard their reputations at the expense of those they might otherwise protect.

The charismatic founder of my organisation, Ray Wyre, used

to suggest that 'children weren't abused by nasty men, they were abused by nice men', a typically provocative but true notion. As the detective suggests, in his forthright way, 'Stranger danger is mostly bollocks.' I think we are drawn, as a society, to the notion of stranger danger, and possibly of sexual abusers being ogres because the alternatives are too painful to manage. Children are abused by men they know, like men we know, who are ostensibly nice.

Grooming has three goals or phases. The first is to make the child feel obligated. This is age dependent, the groomer will offer whatever the child wants, or lacks: love, attention, acclaim, money, alcohol, drugs, accommodation, safety, adventure, opportunity, and so forth. The notion of 'exchange' is misplaced here, children cannot conceive of the contract they are entering, the playing field is tilted away from them.

The creation of obligation is followed by the perpetrator testing the waters: a joke, a wink, an intimacy, a hand here, a pat there, a hug later. Like a ratchet, or like pushing boundaries, the prospective abuser makes conditional what ought not to be conditional, children should be provided with what they need without that being attached to illicit demands. The perpetrator offers, in the main, something apparently normal and prosocial, whilst having antisocial goals in mind. This second phase of grooming, typically, introduces more intrusive physical engagement: touch, molestation, to a child who is silenced because they have been previously led, dishonestly, to believe that they owe something.

The third goal must be to avoid detection, and in the main, detection can be avoided by preventing disclosure. Disclosure can be inhibited by making explicit threats to the personal safety of the child or their family. Such cases are documented. Where gangs of offenders operating in clear sight exist, they have threatened to firebomb the homes of the children they rape. More common, and more subtle, is the simple psychological trick of making the child believe in distorted notions of *we*, *I*, and *you*. Perpetrators suggest '*We* shouldn't be doing this', '*We* might get into trouble', '*We* are having fun'. *I* might be used to suggest '*I* can't help myself', '*I* love you', '*I* got carried away.' *You* might be attached to '*You* led me on', '*You*'re dirty', '*You*'re enjoying this.' These suggestions, like a cognitive virus of sorts, attach and grow in the child's mind: how then does a child disclose something they believe themselves responsible for, or that they feel guilty about?

Leanne's abuse begins in the real world of face to face sexual exploitation, but it continues online. Many children are first engaged in the online world, on social media platforms which are woefully underregulated. Age verification is non-existent, with young children simply able to tick a box which affirms they are over thirteen for many platforms, or over eighteen for sites offering pornographic content. The balance of regulation against freedom will, I suspect, always lean towards the commercial opportunity rather than the social good.

What the digital environment offers, for men with a sexual interest in children, is a world which is effectively free of restraint and oversight. It also provides an environment for children which is exciting and enthralling, yet fraught with risk. On occasions, in offering talks or advice to parents about such matters, I offer a scenario where a random unknown man knocks on their door and asks if he might spend the evening sitting in their son or daughter's bedroom. What might they do? The answer is that they would always say no, or words to that effect, and slam the door in his face. The reality is that many boys and girls spend their evenings, in their own bedrooms, with a host of strangers, some of whom may wish to do them harm, and many parents are oblivious to the fact.

Leanne keeps the true nature of her engagement with Sean

a secret from her mother, holds her phone behind her back, and takes photographs of herself, at his behest, which he then uses to extort more. Sean is in control of Leanne, although he is likely to have suggested, to her, that the conspiracy of silence is a mutual one. The term 'selfie' or 'self-taken image' being used to describe some of this material may hide a multitude of abuses, coercions, extortions, blackmail, and so forth. Many of the men I dealt with who had been arrested for downloading indicated they 'preferred' the selfie, or the supposed selfie; I suspect they could comfort themselves with the notion that apparent compliance could not be underpinned by exploitation.

Leanne does not make a spontaneous disclosure, very few children do. Another child does, during a lesson about such online risks at school. There was a trend, some ten years ago, for children to be shown films based upon real life case studies, where a child succumbed to grooming and was raped or murdered as a result; this would be followed by group discussions and the suggestion, as the mother puts it: 'don't let this happen to you.'

Such inputs have been criticised, quite rightly, for offering essentially pornographic representations of child sexual abuse: where the child is implicitly criticised for making decisions, or 'choices' that were unwise. The implication is that children ought to 'keep themselves safe' or 'avoid danger.' The offerings might veer towards victim blaming, vicariously traumatise those in attendance, or trigger adverse emotional reactions in those children attending who might already have experienced what was being described. Prevention initiatives have tended to be based on the notion that all children are potential victims who ought to safeguard themselves, but this is not balanced out by the notion that all men might be prevailed upon to desist from offending.

When Leanne is interviewed, the implication is that the

'nice man' who she speaks to is the Detective. He had previously described the physical conditions in which she was to be engaged: a building separate from the police station, two cameras, notions of homeliness, and strict protocols in place as to how the interview might be conducted. I have seen state of the art facilities used for these purposes; I have seen buildings that are almost guaranteed to prevent a disclosure. I have seen recordings where children have offered nothing, being too young or too confused, or too ashamed to give anything approaching a credible disclosure. I have seen recordings where the child offers everything up, the interview taking on a therapeutic tone, the perception of being safe and being believed being central to the child's engagement. In Leanne's case, whatever she said would be validated, in a way, by the recordings her abuser had made of his exploitation of her, the police 'had him cold', as the mother puts it.

The reader may be surprised, although by this stage of the book I suspect nothing might surprise any more, that some children who are discovered through the process of victim identification deny that they are represented in the pictures that led to their discovery. The bedroom furniture or bed cover may be the same, the distinctive knickers they had pulled off them may be the same, but the body is not theirs. This denial, or dissociation, or simple embarrassment stems from the power their abuser retains: to suffocate them in a shame that actually belongs to him.

Leanne is spared from the experience of a trial by Sean's admissions, which is doubtless a blessing: some children who have undergone that process describe it as being as traumatic as the abuse itself, which is an astonishing judgement on our systems. Her recovery follows her being persuaded, through therapy, that what took place was not her fault, although that very simple and factual notion is often difficult to convey, since victims' minds are often contaminated

by the offender's world view. Long established, in research, is the fact
that children recover more completely from an abusive experience
when they are believed and supported by their parents. There is
much to learn from that simple fact, although professional hubris
occasionally suggests that a child's recovery rests upon the skills
located in and applied by the system. I conceived of the mother as
an archetype, as someone who simply and unconditionally loved
her child, and who, after various authorities had disengaged, would
'be there' for her, without reserve.

The monologue ends, I hope, hopefully, with the mother singing
a song passed through the generations, a song of unambiguous love
and a chain of connection. My mother in law sang it to my wife,
and my wife to our daughter. Our daughter soon found it 'cringe',
in the vernacular, but I live in hope that, one day, she will sing it
to someone else.

Afterword

I hope the reader of these offerings has been engaged, moved and possibly educated by the experience. I appreciate that sounds a little like the BBC charter or such like, but there you have it. The monologues may be read, or performed, by anyone that wishes to do so. If you intend to do so, please let me know. The intention is that any one of them might spark and inform a conversation about issues that need to be aired.

My organisation, the Lucy Faithfull Foundation, has a website that offers detailed information and advice about many of the issues raised in the monologues and in the notes which accompany them. This may be found, here: https://www.lucyfaithfull.org.uk. Our 'sister' organisation, 'Stop it Now' has public education as part of its remit and hosts much useful content. This is available here: https://www.stopitnow.org.uk

Children Heard and Seen offer a fantastic and innovative service to children whose parents are in prison. They may be found, here: https://childrenheardandseen.co.uk

If you wish to correspond directly, I offer my e-mail here: michael.sheath@yahoo.com

To anyone in any role in safeguarding, and with an eye on my esteemed English A-level teachers at the Boteler Grammar School Warrington, Mrs Wood and Mrs Gaunt, I would quote Yeats, from memory, of course:

'Too long a sacrifice, Can make a stone of the heart.'
Make sure your sacrifices are time limited.

Michael Sheath
June 2022